P9-DDF-503

Man of
Her Dreams

Center Point
Large Print

Also by Tami Hoag and available from
Center Point Large Print:

The 9th Girl

**This Large Print Book carries the
Seal of Approval of N.A.V.H.**

Man of
Her Dreams

TAMI HOAG

CENTER POINT LARGE PRINT
THORNDIKE, MAINE

This Center Point Large Print edition
is published in the year 2014 by arrangement with
Bantam Books, an imprint of Random House,
a division of Random House LLC.

The text of this Large Print edition is unabridged.
In other aspects, this book may vary
from the original edition.
Printed in the United States of America
on permanent paper.
Set in 16-point Times New Roman type.

ISBN: 978-1-62899-229-8

Library of Congress Cataloging-in-Publication Data

Hoag, Tami.
Man of her dreams / Tami Hoag. — Center Point Large Print edition.
pages ; cm
Summary: "A romance classic about a man in love—and the woman
who's determined to prove it to him"—Provided by publisher.
ISBN 978-1-62899-229-8 (library binding : alk. paper)
1. Large type books. I. Title.
PS3558.O333M36 2014
813'.54—dc23
                                                    2014019454

Dear Reader,

Readers often wonder how I got my start as a writer. When I tell them that my first novels were romantic comedies for Bantam's Loveswept line, they're usually quite surprised. Although this genre may seem quite different from the suspense I write now, the two have more in common than it seems.

For me, there are two indispensable elements to every good story: characters to fall in love with and a mystery to be solved—whether it's an unsolved crime or that emotion that perplexes us most of all—love. Even the most sophisticated murder plot can't compare to the intricate and mystifying workings of the human heart.

In *Man of Her Dreams*, Maggie McSwain can't believe that Rylan Quaid is finally proposing to her at his sister's wedding. She'd loved him forever, wanted him desperately. But did he really say that it was time he settled down, and she might as well be the one he settled down with? Maggie refused to be his practical choice for a bride; how could she make her rough-around-the-edges knight admit he adored her?

I loved writing about Maggie and Rylan's fiery relationship years ago, and hope that you'll enjoy them today.

All my best,

Tami Hoag

one

"WELL, HELL." RYLAN Quaid sighed, leaning his elbows on the picnic table. His gray-green eyes were narrowed against the brilliance of the sun slipping over the Blue Ridge Mountains in the distance. He stared at the woman sitting across from him and took a slow, deep breath. "I suppose we could just as well get married."

Maggie McSwain choked on the champagne she'd been drinking to toast her best friend's marriage. The sparkling gold liquid sloshed out of her glass and skittered down the satin bodice of her pink bridesmaid's dress, leaving a dark trail in its wake. She stared at the big man, a wild combination of emotions surging through her: panic, disbelief, soaring joy, and crushing disappointment. "P-pardon me?"

Ry's straight dark brows drew together in irritation. He wasn't a patient man; he didn't like having to ask twice. Now that he'd decided to marry Mary Margaret McSwain, he wanted her to just say yes and have it done with. He stubbornly ignored the ripple of nerves in his stomach. Of course he wasn't nervous, he assured himself. What did he have to be nervous about?

"I said," he drawled with a hint of his

characteristic sarcasm. "I suppose we could just as well get married."

Maggie sat back and stared at him, quite beyond words. Here they were at the wedding reception of her best friend, Rylan's sister, Katie. It had been a glorious day, full of fun and love and romance, and now the man she had secretly loved for years had proposed to her. And she felt as if she'd been hit over the head with a cast iron pan.

What's wrong with this picture, Mary Margaret? she asked herself. *Everything.*

Oh, she had envisioned Rylan Quaid asking her to marry him. She'd fantasized about it a zillion times. Reality was proving to be a trifle less idyllic. Ry had shucked his tux in favor of jeans and a faded denim shirt as soon as they had reached Quaid Farm, where the reception was being held. There was a stain of cocktail sauce on his breast pocket. Not only had he not gotten down on one knee to ask her to marry him, he hadn't even mentioned her name. She wondered wildly if he would have settled for any woman who had happened to sit down across from him. That certainly seemed to be his attitude.

She'd been going out with him for eight weeks. Of course, she had known him for ages. She and Katie Quaid had been friends since their freshman year at William and Mary, nine years ago. Maggie had fallen up to her ears in puppy love the instant she'd laid eyes on her roommate's older brother.

8

Rylan Quaid had been big and masculine and dangerous in a male animal sort of way. He hadn't had the time of day for her, but Maggie had dreamed about him endlessly. She had flunked out of calculus because the only figure she had been able to concentrate on had been Rylan's.

Well, he'd finally taken notice of her. After nine years of dreaming about him and flirting with him, he'd finally asked her out. After eight weeks of dating, he'd asked her to marry him. She should have been ecstatic. She should have been dancing on the table.

She wanted to brain him with the nearest heavy object.

"Let me get this straight, sugar," she said, deceptively calm, her voice all magnolias and honey. "You suppose we could just as well get married?"

Ry grunted, forking up a mouthful of potato salad. He had it all figured out. He wasn't getting any younger. He was thirty-four; it was high time he settled down and had some kids. Maggie was the ideal choice for his wife. She was fun, feisty, willing, and able to stand up to him. Willing to go out with him had been a major prerequisite—he wasn't exactly the most handsome guy in the commonwealth of Virginia.

Maggie wasn't hard to look at either. In fact, he imagined a man could get lost taking in the view of her generous hourglass figure and big brown eyes. He even liked her dark sorrel red hair, which bounced around her head in a perky bob.

They were perfectly suited. Getting married was the practical thing, Ry told himself, deliberately cutting his heart out of the thought process. He had learned long ago to be a practical man. Romance was for poets and idiots and a few lucky people like his sister and her new husband. His one attempt at it had been a miserable disaster, one he wasn't going to repeat.

Certainly he had some tender feelings for Maggie. He cared about her—the way any human being cared for another human being. He was attracted to her—the way any man with eyes in his head would be attracted to her. He would have cheerfully choked any stray male who wandered too close to her.

He wasn't in love with her. He would have sworn up and down he wasn't in love with her. The feelings he experienced around Maggie weren't love, couldn't be love, because he had taken a solemn vow never to fall in love again.

When his mother had walked out on the family, Ry had watched love destroy his father. With stars in his eyes, Tom Quaid had made promises he couldn't keep to a woman who had never wanted his way of life. Bitterness in Joanne had grown and soured and hardened over the years. When she finally walked out, she left her husband desolate.

The man had gone on loving a woman who felt nothing for him but contempt.

Ry had had his own experience with love, or something like it, when he'd been nineteen and just young enough to hope, young enough to want to be proven wrong about love. He'd fallen hard for a girl who was in love with his image as a budding college football star. When he'd been forced to leave school to take over the farm, she had made it abundantly clear that she had been more interested in the football jersey than the man who'd worn it.

Ry had given up on the concept of romantic love then, at least as it pertained to him. He simply wasn't loveable. Women fell in love with men like his horse trainer, Christian Atherton, or Nick Leone, Katie's husband—handsome, charming men, not big rough farmers who didn't have the time or the inclination to be suave and charming.

Love was more trouble than it was worth anyway. As far as he was concerned, marriage was a partnership, and partners needed to be compatible, not in love with each other. Love was too tenuous a thing, too transient. It came and it went. Solid partnerships were enduring.

Maggie sat back and folded her hands on the lap of her champagne-stained dress. Ry hadn't said one word about love. He hadn't even said he *wanted* to marry her. He made it sound as if he had suddenly grown weary of being single and had decided to settle for her instead of looking further. She felt as if she were something being picked out at Kmart because he was too lazy to go across town to a fancier store.

The hurting started around her heart and spread out in ever-widening concentric circles until even her toenails ached. Her hair ached. Her eyelashes ached as she stared at the big, rugged man across the table from her.

He wasn't handsome by movie star standards. Handsome was too tame a word for Rylan Quaid, too pretty a word. The hard, angular planes of his face could have been chiseled from granite. His cheekbones were too high, his gray-green eyes too narrow. He was hardly a slave to fashion, and he combed his dark hair whichever way it happened to be leaning when he got out of bed in the morning. With his bold, high-bridged nose and fierce expression, he made her think of an eagle or some equally predatory creature.

No, he wasn't a handsome man, but he was all man. He was six feet four inches of raw, roped-with-muscle masculinity. Just looking at him made Maggie's blood heat—and she had done little more than look over the past eight weeks. Heaven only knew why. She had certainly wanted to do more than look. The hunger in Ry's kisses at the end of each of their dates had made her think he wanted more too. Yet he hadn't once suggested they go to bed. Nor had he explained why he apparently didn't want to. And now he was asking her to marry him.

Somehow the proposal seemed even more impersonal because they hadn't been intimate— no, it was because he seemed indifferent to the fact that they hadn't been intimate. If he had explained to her that he was old-fashioned and believed in waiting until marriage, she no doubt would have been touched by the secret romantic in him. However, romantic wasn't how he was coming across.

He was coming across as an insensitive, boorish lout. Hardly the man of her dreams. Still, she loved him. She loved him, and it hurt right to the ends of her bobbed red hair.

She didn't want to be the woman he settled for. She wanted to be the woman he'd waited for and loved. She wanted to be the one privileged person he let in behind the steely tough exterior he presented to the rest of the world. In her heart she knew there was something under there besides gristle and orneriness. She wanted to bring out his tender side. She would have laid her heart at his feet if only he had asked.

"You suppose we could just as well get married," she said again quietly. She glanced to her right to see if any of the other wedding guests at their table were witnessing this trampling of her most tender feelings. The other people at the table were engrossed in a spirited discussion about the best way to prepare clams. Maggie felt as if she had swallowed a clam whole. She turned back toward Rylan, who undoubtedly had a clam for a brain.

"Jeepers cripes, Mary Margaret," he said irritably, not willing to admit to himself that he was terrified she was going to say no. Why would he be terrified if he wasn't in love with her? He wouldn't be. He wasn't. "How many times are you going to repeat it? We could have settled on a date and written out half the invitations by now."

Maggie stood up, her temper seething so much that she was certain billowing clouds of steam were rising from her head. "Rylan Quaid, you are the most mannerless, arrogant, unfeeling, boneheaded creature God ever put breath in! I wouldn't have you on a platter, even if they could find one big enough to serve you up on!"

What champagne she hadn't already spilled on her dress went sailing into Rylan's surprised face. Maggie stumbled out from the bench at the picnic table, set on making a grand exit, but the hem of her long rose-colored dress caught on a splinter on the bench, nearly yanking her feet out from under her. The sickening sound of expensive fabric tearing nearly snapped the hair-thin thread of her control. Never in her life had she wanted to burst into tears the way she wanted to right now.

"Son of a sailor," she muttered under her breath, turning back toward the bench. If she started crying and mascara ran all over her face in front of all these people, she was going to publicly flay the hide from that big lummox who now sat staring at her with champagne dripping from the end of his nose. She grabbed the torn hem of her dress and pulled, shortening it from floor-length to tea-length with one good tug.

The rest of the guests at the table dropped their clam debate and turned to stare at Ry and at the stiff retreating back of Maggie McSwain as she marched toward the house.

Watching Maggie storm away, Ry wiped the champagne from his face with his shirtsleeve. Well, that suggestion had gone over like a lead balloon, he thought sourly. He glanced back at the expectant faces of his sister's in-laws and shrugged his mile-wide shoulders.

"It might have been something I said."

Not sparing a glance for any of the people she stalked past, Maggie stomped up the steps, across the wide front porch, and into the big old farmhouse. She was going to find her purse and go home where she could lock herself in her room and bawl her eyes out in private.

How could he do this to her? How could he humiliate her this way? If it had been such a distasteful chore for him to ask her to marry him, he could have waited at least until there weren't two hundred and fifty witnesses to the act.

15

She went through the rambling house, stepping into one room after another, her brain too fuddled to remember where she'd put her purse. Finally she opened a door on someone who was changing clothes.

"Sorry," she mumbled, backing out into the hall.

"Oh, Maggie, come on in," Katie Quaid said, glancing at her friend's reflection in the mirror above the dresser. "Be a darlin' and zip me, will you?"

For a second Maggie didn't move, at a loss as to why Katie was there. Katie. Wedding. For heaven's sake! She'd forgotten all about the wedding. She'd been so immersed in misery over Rylan's behavior, everything else had been pushed from her mind.

Get a hold on yourself, Mary Margaret, this is Katie's big day. No way on earth are you going to spoil it.

She pushed her Cupid's bow mouth up into a smile and walked into the room to where Katie stood with her heavy mane of dark hair lifted out of the way. Katie was as petite as Rylan was enormous. Sometimes it was difficult to remember they were brother and sister.

"How's it going outside?" Katie asked as she applied fresh lipstick. "Is everyone having a good time?"

"Oh . . . you can't imagine," Maggie said brightly, zipping her friend's dress. "There you go. *Hic.*"

Her hand went to her mouth. Her sable brown eyes widened in horror as she met Katie's concerned gaze in the mirror. As quickly as she could, she turned toward the bed and began fussing with the beautiful white satin wedding gown that lay across it. "Don't you worry about this dress, now, y'hear? I'll take it to the cleaners for you first thing Monday morning. *Hic.*"

"Maggie? Maggie, what's wrong?"

She felt Katie's small hand on her shoulder, but she didn't turn around. Terrific, she thought. Caught between a hand-beaded wedding gown and a blushing bride. The need to cry welled up behind her eyes stronger than ever, but she told herself she was not going to cry. She truly was so happy for Katie. She didn't want to do anything to cast a shadow on this day.

"Nothing's wrong," she said on a laugh. Unless you want to count what that big jackass brother of yours just did, she added silently.

Katie planted her hands on her slim hips and narrowed her gray eyes in suspicion. "Mary Margaret McSwain, don't you try to tell me there's nothing wrong. You have the hiccups. After all these years, you think I don't know what it means when you get the hiccups? It means you're upset."

"It means I'm emotional," Maggie corrected. "My best friend just got married—*hic*—something I take much of the credit for. I'm entitled to get a little emotional, aren't I?"

"Well, sure, I—"

"I think I'm entitled to get the *hic* hiccups over that," she went on, turning toward Katie, her brown eyes shimmering with tears. Damnation. She wasn't going to be able to hold them back. It was too much, touching that gorgeous satin wedding dress and seeing Katie glowing with happiness. Getting married was supposed to be like that—wonderfully happy, a time of celebration and love. Rylan probably wouldn't care if she wore a feed sack to this wedding he supposed they could just as well have.

"Maggie?" Katie questioned, her concern plain in her soft low voice.

The dam burst. Maggie wrapped her arms around her friend, crying for all she was worth. Still, she was determined not to upset Katie. "I'm—just—so—happy—for—you!"

The door to the bedroom opened, and Nick Leone stepped in, looking pleasantly impatient and mouth-wateringly handsome in his tux. "Katie, are you ready or what?" Heavy black eyebrows drew together over eyes the color of dark chocolate. "Hey, what's with Maggie?"

Katie looked up at her husband of six hours and said, "She's happy for us."

"Jeez, I'd hate to see her at a funeral."

Maggie disentangled herself from Katie's embrace, sniffling and hiccuping as she tried to wipe the tears from her face and still leave some of her eye makeup intact. Her blurry gaze traveled up the length of Nick Leone. He was one gorgeous hunk of a guy, as sweet as they came, and she had steered Katie his way. She must have had rocks in her head.

Nick had proposed to Katie on one knee in the middle of a crowded restaurant. It had been such a romantic scene, nearly everyone present had cried. Except Rylan, she remembered. Rylan had been more concerned about getting a generous serving of veal scaloppine. How typical.

"*Hic.* You take good care of her, Yankee," she said as Nick engulfed her in a big hug.

"I will," he promised. "And thank you, Maggie. Thank you for forcing Katie to come over to the restaurant to meet me, and thank you for the advice when I thought I'd lost her. We owe you."

If only she could get her own life to work out so well, she thought glumly.

"Oh, go on," she said, stepping out of the circle of his arms. She forced her lips into a smile and waved Nick and Katie toward the door. "Go on. Y'all have a *hic* honeymoon to get to."

"She's right." Nick smiled down at his bride, his dark eyes warm with anticipation.

There was a lingering trace of concern in Katie's gaze as she looked at her friend. "I'll call you as soon as we get back."

Maggie nodded and waved as they disappeared through the door, then sank down on the bed beside Katie's wedding gown. She ran the back of her hand over the tiny seed pearls on the bodice as misery throbbed inside her like a toothache.

She looked up at her reflection in the mirror above the dresser. Her face wasn't going to stop any hearts—neither from awe nor shock. It was sort of heart-shaped. Her chin was a tad too long. Her eyes were her best feature, her nose her worst. She thought it too plain, not feminine enough. She'd always believed she might have had nice cheekbones, except you couldn't see them because of her cheeks.

At any rate, she wasn't unattractive. She hadn't lacked for dates over the years. No doubt she could have found an easier man to fall in love with, but her heart was set on Rylan Quaid.

Now Rylan Quaid had asked her to marry him. But he didn't love her.

They'd had fun together over the last eight weeks, but their dates had been for the most part very casual, often in the company of friends. Much of that time had been spent in a joint effort to mend the rift between Katie and Nick.

The status of her relationship with Ry hadn't really changed since they'd started dating. They'd been friends of a sort for the last five years, ever since she'd moved to Briarwood and she and Katie had gone into business as interior design consultants. She and Ry hadn't been close friends, but the kind who teased and wisecracked.

Now they were a couple, but romance hadn't brought that sensation of everything being new and wonderful and fascinating. Maggie was sure she would have found Rylan fascinating if he hadn't kept her an emotional arm's length away at all times. And Ry seemed to find her about as fascinating as cheddar cheese. He treated her as if she were a comfortable old shoe; she was convenient and familiar, and he'd decided he might as well keep her. He made her feel about as loved as the dozen or so stray dogs that trotted around his farmyard.

Well, a pat on the head and an occasional bone weren't quite what she'd had in mind.

"Bye, princess," Ry said, giving his sister a hug and helping her into Nick's Trans Am. "Have a nice time in Williamsburg."

"We will." Katie smiled up at him. "Take care of Maggie."

"Yeah. Sure," he muttered as the wine-colored sports car rolled down the driveway. Behind him the rest of the wedding guests were talking and laughing as they filed back toward the festivities on the lawn. He stood there for several minutes scuffing his boots on the gravel.

He had planned on taking care of Maggie. There was just one small hitch—she'd all but told him to go take a flying leap. That wasn't the reaction he had imagined getting from her. Maggie could be

21

as silly as the next woman, but most of the time she was practical. Didn't she see the sense in his plan?

Maybe not, he decided, sipping his beer thoughtfully. He had taken her by surprise with his proposal. Maybe what she needed was to discuss the logic of marrying him. He reached a hand up and rubbed the back of his sunburned neck. Yeah, that was what he'd do. He would calmly explain to her why they should get married, she would see reason, then he would outline the plan. Simple.

"Maggie, I think we need to talk," he said, intercepting her at her car. His hand encircled her upper arm. Sandwiched between the car and the car door, she glared up at him with brown eyes rimmed in red and black. Ry grimaced. "Crimeny, you look like a hung-over raccoon."

"Thank you for *hic* pointing that out to me, Rylan." She nearly spat the words up at him. "Did they teach you that in charm school?"

Another layer peeled away from his thin supply of patience. "For Pete's sake, Mary Margaret, what's gotten into you? I asked you to marry me. Hell, you're acting like I just handed you a dead fish or something."

She gave him a disgusted look. "You have a way with words that would make Shakespeare throw up."

"Well, since he's been dead a few hundred years. I'm not gonna worry about it." He turned and headed toward the long white stables with Maggie in tow. A coon hound, a half-grown collie, and a cocker spaniel trotted after them.

"I wouldn't be following you"—Maggie was jogging to keep up with his long strides and her pink satin pumps were scuffed on the rocks— "but I happen to *hic* use that arm every once in a while. So where are you dragging me and for what purpose?"

"We need to have a discussion, and I'd just as soon not have half of Briarwood listening in."

"*Now* he wants privacy," she muttered to herself.

Ry let go of her once they were in the paneled office of the stable. He leaned back against his big oak desk, motioned Maggie to a chair, and crossed his arms over his massive chest.

"I'd rather *hic* stand, thank you," she said primly, crossing her own arms and looking down at the jagged hemline of her dress. It probably would be a more practical dress this way, she told herself, trying to console herself over the ruination of what had been the most beautiful creation she'd ever worn.

Ry shrugged, his nervousness coming across as indifference. "Suit yourself. I thought we should talk over this marriage business a little more. You didn't seem to agree with me." He watched for her reaction from the corner of his eye as he scratched at the stain on his shirt pocket.

"Oh?" Maggie's brows lifted in mock innocence. "What gave you that idea? Was it the names I called you or the champagne I threw in your face?"

"A little of both, I'd say." He frowned, picked up a pencil, and rolled it between his fingers. "I don't understand your reaction. I asked you to marry me. I thought women generally wanted to get married. I thought—"

"Why?" Maggie asked. She didn't want to stand and listen to Ry's philosophy of women. She wanted to cut to the heart of the matter and ask the sixty-four-thousand-dollar question. The odds were probably astronomical against him giving the answer she wanted to hear, but she had to ask.

Ry looked baffled and a little annoyed at the interruption. "Why? Why what?"

"Why did you ask me to *hic* marry you?" The drum roll began in her head.

"Because," he started. A strange feeling wiggled around in his stomach. He couldn't quite identify it. It must have been the shrimp cocktail.

Why had he asked Maggie McSwain to marry him? Well, the answer to that was simple, he told himself. Practical. His mind latched onto the word like a hound on a bone. That was why— practicality. Right. It really didn't have that much to do with the way his palms sweated when his gaze lingered on her full breasts—that was a bonus. And it didn't have anything to do with the way she looked at him after he kissed her—as if he had been transformed from a frog into Prince Charming. That look was something he didn't want to know anything about, probably because it caused his heart to flutter, and the last thing he needed was a fluttering heart. Practicality was his motto.

He shook a finger at her. "This is exactly what I wanted to talk to you about. We make a good team. We're compatible, complementary. I think we're both at an age when it's time to settle down—might as well be with each other."

"Might as well be with each other," she repeated, though it really was more a matter of lip-syncing than speaking. The anticipatory drum roll in her head ended with a noisy clashing of cymbals. The din made her ears ring. "Amazing."

"It makes sense," Ry said, not quite able to decipher Maggie's expression. She hadn't thrown anything at him, so he had to be on the right track. "It's the practical thing."

"The practical thing."

Ry's formidable scowl snapped into place, his lips thinning to a hard line above his rock-solid jaw. "Gosh almighty, Mary Margaret, you're starting to sound just like a damn parrot."

"Maybe you ought to buy yourself a *hic* parrot then, sugar," Maggie said sharply, "if you're looking for companionship in your old age." She began to pace the width of the room, which smelled of leather, horses, and dust.

"I don't want companionship. I want a wife."

Maggie threw her hands in the air. "Now there's a gem!"

"I want a wife and a family," Ry went on, ignoring her sarcasm. "I can't have a family by myself."

"Oh, but you could try," she said with a malicious smile.

Lord, was he truly so blind he couldn't see it? All these years she'd been in love with him, and he really didn't have a clue? Maggie shook her head. No, she hadn't made it plain that she was in love with him. She'd kept it to herself for a long time because he hadn't seemed interested in her. But she had hoped once he asked her out things would progress.

Things had progressed all right. Things had progressed to the point that she wanted to tear his head off and use it for a bowling ball.

"Rylan," she said, trying to muster some patience. She stopped her pacing and took a deep breath. "People start IRA's because it's practical."

"I know," he said absently, his gaze involuntarily riveted on the rise and fall of her cleavage. "I've got one."

"Figures." She turned her head and stared in the direction of the photographs on the wall, photographs of the horses Ry raised. They were pictures of his show jumpers winning at some of the most prestigious horse shows in the world.

To Maggie the pictures were nothing more than squares with blobs of color on them; her concentration was elsewhere.

Ry's frustration came out in a humorless laugh. "I don't understand the problem here, Maggie. I've listed every perfectly good reason for us to get married. What more do you want from me?"

Maggie closed her eyes on her tears. All she'd ever wanted since she'd been a goofy freshman at William and Mary was for Rylan Quaid to fall in love with her. But he couldn't have cut those words out of her with a knife. If she couldn't have Ry's love, she would at least hang on to her pride.

She lifted her chin and gave him a belligerent stare. "I won't have you propose to me simply because I'm convenient. I'm an admiral's daughter, dammit, not some brood mare you picked up cheap at an auction. So you can take your offer on an extended honeymoon, Rylan Quaid, because I wouldn't marry you if you were the last man in the cosmos!"

Ry kicked the side of his desk and let loose a string of expletives as his office door slammed shut. He flung himself into his creaky old desk chair, planted his elbows on the ink blotter, and raked his fingers back through his dark hair. They'd hit the root of the problem, hadn't they?

She was an admiral's daughter, and when you came right down to it, he wasn't anything more than a farmer. His crop might have been animals with price tags that ran into six figures, but that didn't keep him from sweating and getting dirt under his fingernails. The truth was, Maggie didn't think he was good enough for her.

She'd probably only gone out with him because she thought he was rich. Most people did think that. On paper he *was* rich, but everything he had was tied up in the farm, in the horses. He worked from sunup to sundown to keep the place in the black.

It had been a long, hard struggle to get Quaid Farm to the point it was now. When his father died, Ry had been going to the university in Charlottesville on a football scholarship. His dream had been to become a veterinarian. Instead, he'd inherited a huge debt and a load of responsibility.

A lot of dreams had died and been buried along with Tom Quaid. One had surfaced—to build the farm up into one of the finest in the country. He had done that. Many of the best horses in the national and international show rings had been bred and raised at Quaid Farm. At the top of the list was his own stallion, Rough Cut, who would soon be retired from competition and syndicated to stand at stud.

With a sardonic smile twisting his lips, Ry wondered if Maggie would find him acceptable as a husband once she heard the amount of money Rough Cut had been syndicated for. He would be rich then. No doubt women would be lining up to marry him.

Oddly that idea didn't appeal to him. He wanted Maggie McSwain. He'd spent too many years as a horse breeder not to know a good cross when he saw one. Maggie might have her irrational female moments, but she was his match in every way. She wasn't afraid of hard work. She wasn't afraid to stand toe to toe with him in a shouting match. She had a body that tempted him until he didn't trust himself to get within three feet of her. She had a nurturing quality that would make her a wonderful mother.

All he had to do was close his eyes and he could see her nursing his baby son at her beautiful, ripe breast. The scene brought a surge of warmth to his heart and his loins. Opening his eyes, he denied both feelings and set his mind to the task at hand.

He wanted Maggie McSwain for his bride, and he was going to do whatever he needed to get her.

Everything short of falling in love.

two

THE LONG, TREE-LINED drive of Poplar Grove Plantation was a welcome sight, until Maggie pulled her car into the parking area and realized that the last of the day's tourists had yet to go home. Half a dozen cars were parked there. Now, not only was she going to have to get past her landladies in her torn dress and tearstained face, she was also going to have to negotiate her way through a crowd of strangers. Lovely.

She gazed at the brick Georgian mansion with its twin chimneys and two-story pillared portico. It had been a case of love at first sight between her and the old house that was situated only a mile outside of Briarwood. The elderly sisters whose family had owned Poplar Grove for eight generations had been in need of a boarder. Maintaining a two-hundred-year-old showplace was an expensive business. The ladies were living on meager retirement funds and the money garnered from giving guided tours of the house, but that had left little extra for the work that was necessary to maintain it.

It had been an ideal situation for Maggie, who specialized in historical preservation and restoration in her decorating work. Poplar Grove and the Darlington sisters—Miss Emma Darlington and Mrs. Betsy Darlington-Claiborne—had offered pleasant companionship, the home of her dreams, and an opportunity to work at preserving a piece of history.

Of course, the arrangement wasn't without its pitfalls. Privacy was sometimes hard to come by. She and the ladies lived on the second floor. The first floor was often crawling with tourists, being open to the public daily, year-round. And Miss

Emma and Mrs. Claiborne, while darling ladies that Maggie had grown to love, seldom minded their own business. Miss Emma said they were at an age when they didn't have to worry about propriety, that old ladies were entitled to be snoopy and say whatever they wanted.

If she were very lucky, Maggie thought, pulling her square black sunglasses out of her purse and slipping them on to cover her puffy, red-rimmed eyes, both ladies would be in the dining room with the tour group, telling them the story of how their grandmother saved the family silver during The War by dumping it in a gunny sack and sinking it in the well. She really wasn't in the mood to give a play-by-play account of what had happened between herself and Rylan at the reception.

She wanted to get to her room so she could start planning her strategy. If Rylan Quaid thought he could propose to her like that and get away with it, he was sadly mistaken. Even now she was envisioning the successful resolution of her upcoming campaign, the way a general envisions his opponent surrendering on the field of battle. Yes, she could see it now: Rylan Quaid on his knees, pouring his heart out, proclaiming his love for her, begging her to marry him and put him out of his misery.

Just as she started up the wide front steps, the double doors swung open wide, and a dozen tourists filed out onto the porch. They were followed by a pair of diminutive gray-haired ladies, their hostesses, Miss Emma and Mrs. Claiborne, who wore cotton print dresses with the snug bodices and long, full skirts that had been popular in colonial times.

Miss Emma took one look at Maggie and pressed a hand to her mouth as if to keep from blurting out something imprudent in front of their guests. Mrs. Claiborne didn't bat an eyelash. Twitching her long skirt aside, she descended one step, took Maggie's limp hand in hers, and led her up to the center of the group.

"This is Ms. McSwain," she said in a perfectly modulated voice of a true Southern lady, "our resident expert on historical preservation."

If she hadn't been so miserable, Maggie would have smiled at the title that made her sound like a paid consultant instead of a boarder. She hiccupped and nodded a greeting to the people who were stealing glances at the frayed bottom of her dress.

As Mrs. Claiborne ushered her into the house, she heard Miss Emma comment in her sweet way, "Darlin' girl, and simply amazin'. She's blind as a bat, you know."

When they reached the parlor on the second floor, Mrs. Claiborne released Maggie's arm and broke the silence with a harmless-sounding question. "How was the reception?"

Maggie searched for an appropriate word as she

watched her landlady go to the mahogany Queen Anne serving table and pour a shot of bourbon from a crystal decanter that dated back to the War of 1812. "Oh . . . memorable. If you'll excuse me, Mrs. Claiborne, I believe I'll *hic* go change."

As she turned to go, Miss Emma charged to the top of the steps, across the hall, and into the room, her long dress hiked up to her knees, revealing a pair of high-top Reeboks on her tiny feet. "What have I missed?" she asked breathlessly, tucking back a strand of hair that had escaped her bun. Her bright blue eyes focused on Maggie, taking in the mussed hair, sunglasses, and ruined dress. "That must have been one hell of a party, sugar."

"It was certainly eventful," Maggie said dryly.

Miss Emma looked accusingly at her twin sister. "See there. I told you we should have stayed for the reception." She turned back to Maggie. "Did anyone steal the bride? How about the groom? I'd'a paid money to be in on that. That Nick Leone is enough to give me a hot flash."

Mrs. Claiborne snorted as she crossed the Aubusson carpet with the tumbler of bourbon. "You get a hot flash over anything in pants. I think you ought to get your hormones checked."

Miss Emma dismissed the notion with a wave of her dainty hand. "Sister, at seventy-four we ought to thank the Almighty that we still have hormones."

"Speak for yourself. I wore mine out twenty years ago."

Deciding to take advantage of their friendly bickering, Maggie started backing toward the door. "I'm bushed, ladies. I believe I'll go to my *hic* room."

Immediately the hormone debate subsided. Working as a team, the ladies piloted Maggie to a blue damask wing chair and commanded her to sit. Mrs. Claiborne pressed the whiskey glass into her hand as Miss Emma pulled her sunglasses off.

"Lord have mercy, you look like a hung-over raccoon."

Maggie scowled at Miss Emma's choice of analogies.

"This undoubtedly has something to do with Rylan Quaid," Mrs. Claiborne pronounced, crossing her arms over her meager bosom.

Squirming in her chair, Maggie contemplated lying to them, but one look at Mrs. Claiborne's expression told her she'd never pull it off. She took a sip of the bourbon. Her throat burned, her eyes watered. Hoarsely she said, "He asked me to marry him."

"Yahoo!" Miss Emma whooped, clapping her hands. "Snatch him up, sugar. He ain't Tom Cruise, but he's some big hunk of man. I'd take him in a minute."

"You'd take the mailman if he lingered at the box long enough," Mrs. Claiborne said disgustedly. "Emma, can't you see this isn't good news?"

Miss Emma made a face. She went to the narrow

table along the paneled wall, poured herself a bourbon, and tossed it back. "She's been moonin' over Rylan Quaid for years. He finally asks her to marry him. How can that *not* be good news?"

"He doesn't love me," Maggie said, trying to ignore the sting of those words. "We've only been dating for eight weeks. We haven't even—er—um—*hic*—" Her cheeks flushed hotly to a shade of pink that clashed with her dress. She hadn't meant to bring *that* up. "That is to say . . ."

"Oh, dear," Miss Emma said, rubbing her chin thoughtfully. "That is bad. A big strappin' man like him. You don't suppose he's gay, do you?"

"I don't suppose he'd be asking Mary Margaret to marry him if he was gay, Emma. He'd be asking that handsome rake of a horse trainer that works for him."

"True." Miss Emma plopped down on the needlepoint footstool at Maggie's feet, her voluminous skirt spreading out around her. With a sympathetic look, she took Maggie's free hand in hers. "Spill your guts, McSwain."

Maggie resigned herself. Sooner or later the Darlington sisters were going to weasel the truth out of her. "Rylan thinks getting married would be the practical thing to do."

"And he picked you to do it with." Miss Emma winced. "Pardon the expression."

Maggie shook her head, fresh anger lighting up her dark eyes as she recalled Ry's offhand attitude. "He settled for me. It was one of those right-place-at-the-right-time things. I won't marry a man who doesn't love me."

"So, that's the end of it," Mrs. Claiborne said sadly.

Maggie handed Miss Emma her half-empty whiskey tumbler and stood up. She tossed the sisters a look burning with challenge. "The hell it is."

When she caught sight of her reflection in the large mirror above her dresser, she grimaced and groaned aloud. "Sugar, you *do* look like a hung-over raccoon."

Her bridesmaid's dress hit the floor and stayed there in a crumpled heap. Clad only in her slip, she flopped down on the double-wedding-ring quilt that covered her four-poster bed and stared at the enormous stuffed brown bear that sat on a wicker stool beside her nightstand.

She had found the fuzzy toy in a shop in Williamsburg the week after she had first met her best friend's brother. Big and burly with a comically disgruntled expression, it had reminded her of Rylan to such an extent that she'd blown a whole month's spending money on it. In those days she had gone to sleep every night dreaming of the day she could have the real Ry in her room instead of Randy the bear, his furry facsimile.

"Be careful what you wish for, Mary Margaret, you just might get it," she mumbled to herself.

She had wished for Rylan Quaid. The trouble was, over the years her romantic imagination had created a secret persona for Ry, one he revealed only to her. In her dreams he was a man of great tenderness, a man who adored her, who composed love ballads for her and read poetry to her. She had spent plenty of time with her imaginary Ry until the real article had finally gotten around to asking her out. And when he had, she had promptly discovered he wasn't precisely the man of her dreams.

In most ways Ry was exactly what he appeared to be—a big, gruff farmer. He was rough around the edges, wouldn't have known charm if it spit in his face. In other ways he was full of surprises. He was a wine connoisseur. He read classic literature. He had a dry, acerbic wit that could carve stone.

Maggie was still convinced there was a deeper, secret side to Rylan, but he hadn't revealed it to her. He didn't write poetry that she knew of, and he didn't adore her. But she was in love with him. As hurt and angry as she was, she loved him.

She was too tired to fight the feeling off, too tired to keep from fantasizing that he was lying next to her on the bed, his big, calloused hands running over her fevered skin as he whispered promises of ecstasy to her. She closed her eyes and smiled as she imagined the wonderful, hot words he would murmur in her ear as their legs tangled and their bodies arched together.

A sigh ribboned out of her, mingled with the softest of moans as a knock sounded on her door. It probably was Mrs. Claiborne with supper and a lecture to eat it, Maggie thought.

Not even bothering to sit up, she called out, "Come in."

Ry hesitated. Even though Miss Emma had practically come right out and said Maggie was waiting for him to put it an appearance, he felt uncomfortable going into her bedroom. He'd demonstrated the patience of a saint over the past weeks, but seeing Maggie in her own bedroom could push him over the edge. That was all he needed—another strike against him in her book.

Want of her was a living ache in his gut. He'd never wanted a woman so badly in his life. He had hoped to hold off until she was married to him, thinking that once she was his, all legal and proper, maybe he would have enough control to keep from jumping on her like a raving madman.

Every time she came near him, he felt his control slip. Every time he kissed her, it went up in smoke as quickly as burning cellophane. Every time he touched her, images flashed through his head of burying himself in her, taking her hard and fast to relieve the ache in his gut and cool the fire in his blood.

That scenario didn't appeal to the civilized part of him, and he was convinced it wouldn't appeal to Maggie either. She would want soft words, silk sheets, and a suave lover, a man with the patience and tact to be gentle, to go slowly. To complicate matters further, Ry was well aware of his own size and strength. If he took Maggie the way his libido demanded every time he caught a whiff of her perfume, he would hurt her and she'd hate him and he'd never get her to the altar.

When he pushed her door open, his breath hardened like cement in his lungs. Maggie was stretched out across the bed in a white silk slip. Her eyes were closed. She stretched like a cat, the slip gliding over her lush curves with a whisper. One strap dropped over her shoulder as she turned onto her side, allowing the cup to gape away from the ripe fullness of her breast.

Ry groaned inwardly, muttering a string of words under his breath that were a combination of cursing and prayer for deliverance. Trying unsuccessfully to tear his gaze from the erotic picture she presented and focus on the painting above her, he checked his desire ruthlessly.

"I take it you're not still mad at me."

Maggie's eyes snapped open at the dryly drawled words. She gasped, sitting bolt upright on the bed, unaware that her slip climbed up her thighs as she did so. She grabbed a pillow and held it across her breasts. "Rylan! What are you doing here?"

"You invited me in," he pointed out, unable to tear his gaze away from the top of her stocking and the tab of her frilly white garter belt that peeked out from where the hem of her slip had ridden up. His fingers itched to unsnap that tab and roll the nylon down her shapely leg.

"I wan't expecting it to be you!" she said.

Though he refused to recognize it for what it was, a surge of jealousy burned through his desire. His look was ferocious. "Just who were you expecting?"

"Mrs. Claiborne," Maggie said, yanking up the strap of her slip. "I couldn't possibly have known you were coming here."

"That's not what Miss Emma told me." To save Maggie's virtue and his own sanity, he snatched her robe off the post at the end of the bed and thrust it at her. "Put this on before you catch your death."

Maggie grabbed the black kimono out of his hand. Standing up, she turned her back to him, rammed her arms into the sleeves, and belted it with an angry tug on the sash that almost forced the breath out of her. Nothing like adding insult to injury, she thought. Not only did he not love her, he didn't even want to look at her. Damn the man.

"Ooooh, Miss Emma. That stinker. She sent you in here on purpose."

"She said you were expecting me."

"And you believed her? Everyone knows she tells the most outrageous fibs." She sat back down on the bed, crossed her arms and legs, and huffed impatiently. "Why, I wouldn't be at all surprised to hear she told you I was up here having erotic dreams about you when I'm so mad I could spit tacks."

The sarcastic statement brought a telltale flush to the apples of her cheeks, but Ry didn't notice. He had a plan to concentrate on.

"I came to apologize for this afternoon," he said, abruptly changing the subject. "I guess I upset you a little bit."

Maggie rolled her eyes. "Your talent for understatement is truly astonishing."

"Well, I just thought we ought to clear the air." He wandered to her dresser and idly examined the various articles that cluttered the top, all the while keeping one eye on her via the mirror. "To tell you the truth, Maggie, I don't know what got into me today. I suppose with Katie getting married and all, I was carried away."

"Carried away?" she murmured, her stomach fluttering with sudden nerves.

Ry picked up an eyelash curler and played with it absently. "Well, sure. My baby sister's married now, I ought to be married too. You know, it's sort of a reflex action. I reckon there are all sorts of deeper psychological ramifications, but—"

"Just what are you saying, Rylan?" Maggie asked, her eyes narrowing in suspicion.

"Basically that I never should have proposed to you today." He maintained a poker face while he watched Maggie's reaction. She was utterly still on the bed, her face milk white.

"You shouldn't have?" she asked weakly. Even worse than having him propose the way he had was having him say he shouldn't have done it at all.

A flash of panic went through her like a lightning bolt. Dammit, she should have snatched him up when she'd had the chance, married him, and *then* gotten him to fall in love with her. Now they were back to square one.

"No," he went on calmly, trying to pull the eyelash curler off his fingers. It crashed onto a mirrored tray. He righted a bottle of nail polish and picked up a tube of lipstick to fiddle with. "Of course, that was obvious from your reaction. You were right, we're not ready to get married. I take my proposal back."

"But I never—" She bit her tongue, ran a hand back through her hair, and tried to gather her scattering thoughts. She had never said they weren't ready to get married, but she *had* said she *wouldn't* marry him. So what was the difference? "Not ready" left the situation open at least. But who did he think he was, taking his proposal back? How could he retract a proposal she'd already thrown back in his face?

None of this was making any sense to her. The only thing that was clear was the anger building to the boiling point inside her once again. How dare he jerk her feelings around as if she were some kind of puppet!

Ry watched as twin spots of magenta appeared on her cheeks then spread out to the roots of her hair. *Right on cue,* he smiled to himself, *here comes that infamous McSwain temper.* He turned just in time to ward off the pillow she flung at him.

"You colossal jerk!" she shouted, launching herself off the bed as she heaved her pillow at him. With nothing else to throw at him within easy reach, she stamped her bare foot on the pine floor. "First you publicly insult me with a half-assed proposal, now you think you can take it back?"

Ry tried to look innocent. Inwardly he was praising the concept of reverse psychology. It was the perfect tool to use on women, since their minds tended to function in direct opposition to logic. His was a brilliant plan. If Maggie thought he didn't want to get married, she was liable to all but drag him to the altar. He would lure her with indifference and cement the deal with the syndication money.

He was projecting a Thanksgiving wedding.

He lifted his broad shoulders in a hesitant shrug as she continued to glare at him, magnificent in her anger. "I suppose if you had changed your mind, you could hold me to it. I mean, I did make the offer in front of witnesses. Have you changed your mind?"

"No!"

"Good—"

"Good? Good!" She cast a longing glance at his shins. If only she were wearing shoes! She grabbed the lipstick tube out of Rylan's hand and shook it at him as if she could kill him with it. "Ooooh! When it comes to thick-skinned, dirt-for-brains men, you absolutely steal the prize, Rylan Quaid! Good? What do you mean, good? If you had one molecule of gentlemanliness in you, you'd know enough to pretend at least a little bit of disappointment when a lady turns down your proposal!"

Ry held his hands up in surrender. "Now don't go getting all riled up again, Mary Margaret. All I meant was you and I have a good thing going. Why ruin it by getting married?"

"Ruin—?" She heaved a sigh and shook her head. "You have an extremely twisted view of marriage."

"I haven't seen many sterling examples."

Immediately Maggie backed off from the fight. She knew all about Ry and Katie's parents. Their mother had walked out on the family. Katie rarely spoke of the woman, but Maggie was well aware of the effect the desertion had had on her friend. Somehow she had never thought of it as having influenced Ry. He was so big and strong. Now she could see she'd been wrong. She could also see, in his simple answer, a tiny glimpse of that

44

man she had dreamed lay under Ry's abrasive exterior.

Growing up in an environment of hostility had tainted his view of marriage as much as having his mother abandon them had. No wonder he had approached the subject from the practical point of view. That would be the safest way—no emotional risk.

"Do you think getting married will ruin Katie and Nick's relationship?" she asked.

"No. What they have is special," he said quietly, turning once again to browse through her cosmetics. He knew his sister and her husband were in love—deeply, irrevocably in love. He also knew it was something that could never happen for him. He couldn't inspire those kinds of feelings in a woman. The best he hoped for in a relationship was understanding, friendship, and fidelity. "What they have is rare."

We could have it too, Ry, Maggie thought, her heart aching.

"So," he said, accidentally squirting himself with cologne. He swore under his breath and put the atomizer down. "What do you say, Mary Margaret? Can we go on being friends and forget I ever mentioned marriage?"

She nibbled her lush lower lip as she considered his question. Whether he realized it or not, what Ry was offering her was a prime second chance, a chance to make him fall in love with her, a chance to change his mind about marriage. She would have been lying to say she didn't want that chance.

Sure, he was hardheaded and thick-skinned. Sure, he made her angry. No one could rile her the way Rylan could, that was part of what she loved about him.

She could cling to her pride and spite herself by refusing his offer of "just friends," or she could seize the opportunity and make the most of it. Deliberation wasn't necessary.

Determination filled her previously weary body with strength. She was through waiting for Rylan to make all the moves. She would do everything she could to capture his interest, to make him see her love was a prize to be cherished instead of settled for. And she was finished with resigning herself to nothing more than a hot good-night kiss. "Just friends" was going to last only as long as it took her to work her feminine wiles on him. The next time Rylan Quaid asked her to marry him, practicality would be the last thing on his mind.

She met his expectant gaze in the mirror, offering him a reluctant smile. Slowly she stepped closer to him and slid her arms around his waist. She rested her cheek against his broad, muscled back, breathing in his warm, masculine scent. Miss Emma was right, he was some hunk of man. And he was going to be all hers.

"I guess we can still be friends," she said, deliberately ignoring the second half of his question.

Ry swallowed hard at the feeling of her breasts pressing softly into his back. There was a hint of strain in his voice when he spoke. "I'm glad you're being so adult about this, Maggie. A lot of women wouldn't be."

"Well, sugar," she said, slipping around to wedge herself between Ry and her dresser. She tilted her head just so and batted her lashes at him in a manner that was patently seductive. "I'm not a lot of women."

But you're a lot of woman, he thought, fighting back a groan as his palms started to sweat. Her robe had worked loose, and he now had an unobstructed view of her cleavage.

"We should seal this bargain, don't you think?" she said, plucking her nail buffer from his fingers and dropping it behind her. "Kiss and make up?"

"A handshake is all you need dealin' horses," he said with a nervous laugh. Her belly was pressing softly, provocatively against his hardening groin. He wanted her so badly, he could barely think straight. He had to remember they weren't alone in the big house, had to remember he couldn't make love to her until he had a firm handle on his control, or he was liable to ruin his grand plan.

Maggie slid her arms up around his neck, tingles running through her at the tightening of his heavy

47

muscles. Her voice was low and smooth as she raised on tiptoe and inched her mouth toward his. "We aren't dealin' horses, sugar. Besides, what's a lil' old kiss between *friends?*"

The kiss was hot. There was no gradual warming. It was hot from the first. Maggie's lips coaxed and teased. Her tongue sought and gained entry to Ry's mouth, then retreated, luring him to sample the sweet delights of hers. He needed no more encouragement. Crushing her in his embrace, he took control of his kiss and lost control of his desire. His hand slid down her back to cup her bottom. There was a clatter of things falling on the dresser as he lifted her against him and slanted his mouth across hers.

Lack of oxygen was the only thing that saved him from taking her right there on the cluttered dresser. He tore his lips from hers to drag in a ragged breath, and a measure of sanity rushed in with it. He fought off a vague sense of panic and congratulated himself. Why should he feel as if he had been tactically outmaneuvered? He was the one with the plan, and the plan was working.

Putting an inch of space between them, he shot her a rare grin and said, "Well, that ought to seal the deal. Friends again."

Friends indeed, Maggie thought, fighting a smile of smug satisfaction. A man couldn't kiss like that and be indifferent. Indifference didn't strain against the front of a man's jeans. This scheme of hers was going to work out fine. And the beauty of it was Rylan would never figure out he'd been manipulated. Men were so dense about that sort of thing.

Mischief sparkled in her dark eyes as she caught a whiff of the perfume he'd accidentally sprayed on the front of his denim shirt. She reached for the top button. "Mercy, Rylan, you smell like an Avon Lady. Why don't you let me take this shirt and wash it for you?"

Ry caught her hands as the third button and buttonhole parted company and his shirt opened further to reveal a vee of bronze skin thickly carpeted with curling black hair. Maybe his plan was working a little too well. "That's not necessary."

"Oh, pooh," Maggie said, trying not to giggle. "It's no trouble a'tall. Besides, what will the boys in the stable think if you come around smelling like Passion's Promise?"

"Passion's Promise?" He scowled. "Hell of a name for perfume."

"I think it's very appropriate." She lifted her wrist and brushed it in a slow, sensuous caress against his beard-shadowed cheek, knowing by the way his nostrils flared that he was inhaling the seductive scent. She ran her tongue along her kiss-ripened lower lip. "Don't you think so?"

"I think," he said firmly, taking another step back from her, "that I'd better get home. It's chore time, and I still have a yard full of people from New Jersey to see to."

"Oh. Well, if you're sure." She allowed herself a tiny smile as she glanced down and tightened the sash of her kimono. This day wasn't turning out so bad after all. She looked up as Ry started for the bedroom door. "Rylan?"

The look he shot her with his stormy gray-green eyes bordered on suspicious. "What?"

She gave him a genuine smile. "I'm glad we're friends again."

"Me too," he said, although he had the distinct feeling they had just declared an odd kind of war. It was a ridiculous idea, he told himself, and immediately dismissed it. It was his plan, he was in control of the situation. He turned and took a step before her voice stopped him again.

"Ry?"

"What?"

"Better button your shirt, darlin'. You'll give Miss Emma palpitations. She's hot for your bod, you know." She couldn't help but laugh at the look he gave her as he took her advice. "It's true!"

Ry's voice rang with disapproval. "Miss Emma is a sweet little seventy-some-year-old lady—"

"—who has eyes for a big strappin' man." Maggie waggled her eyebrows suggestively and held back her laughter as Ry blushed with embarrassment.

"Good evening, Mary Margaret," he said in a tone that hinted at exasperation.

She waved to him as he walked out. "Good night, *friend.*"

Maggie listened as Ry's boots clomped down the hall and descended the stairs. She sat on the ledge of her window and watched him walk away from the house to his blue-and-gray pickup truck.

He was rough around the edges, but he had the makings of a real fine man. Her man.

"I'll get you to love me, Rylan Quaid," she said with quiet determination, "or die trying."

three

THAT SHE WAS going to die trying was beginning to look like a definite possibility.

Maggie stood in the wide aisle of Quaid Farm's main barn looking up, up, up at the horse she had so cavalierly said she would ride. It was all a part of her brilliant—but seriously flawed—plan: Ry was more likely to fall in love with her if they spent a lot of time together. It followed that he would be impressed if they spent some of that time enjoying his favorite pursuits. He loved to ride; therefore, she would love to ride. But that was where the plan hit a snag.

Maggie didn't love to ride. Horses terrified her. The few experiences she'd had with the beasts had been unpleasant. She hadn't even liked riding the merry-go-round as a child. Once, at a fair in Norfolk, her father had taken her to the pony ring. The pony she was to ride had taken one look at her, pinned back its little ears, and bit her. These were memories that had remained conveniently buried in her subconscious when she had suggested to Rylan that they go riding together. They all came rushing to the fore now that she was standing next to the big brown gelding Ry had selected for her.

"What's his name?" she asked as he snugged up the girth on her saddle.

He tugged on a billet strap, dropped the saddle flap down, and gave the horse an affectionate smack on the side. "Killer."

Maggie's face dropped. In a voice as thin as gossamer she asked, "Why?"

Ry rolled his eyes as he started across the aisle toward his own mount. "It's a misnomer, a joke. It's a wonder he swats flies, he's so gentle. If he was any quieter, he'd be dead."

"Oh." Hesitantly she reached a hand toward the horse's muzzle. The gelding touched her fingertips, flared his wide nostrils, and snorted. With a little yelp, Maggie bolted backward, slamming into Rylan's chest. His hands came up to cup her shoulders.

"Are you sure you want to do this, Mary Margaret?"

"Absolutely!"

It wasn't going to further her cause any to have Ry know she was afraid of horses. Horses were his life. He wasn't going to want a wife who wouldn't share that with him. She was simply going to have to overcome her fear. Literally dragging her feet, she inched toward Killer, reaching out to pat his shoulder, careful to stay an arm's length away. "I love riding, but it's been a little while since I've done it, that's all."

"Like in another lifetime." Ry chuckled under his breath, shaking his head in amusement.

A little smile tugged at his firm lips. She really was too darn cute in her brand-new riding togs. The buffcolored breeches hugged her well-rounded derriere. Her tall, polished brown boots had yet to get a scuff mark on them. She was now regarding Killer with a look of determination that said she was going to ride this horse if for no other reason than that she had spent about two hundred and fifty bucks on the outfit.

She's playing right into your hands, old boy, he told himself, resisting the urge to grin. Maggie had never shown the least interest in riding until he'd retracted his proposal. Now, all of a sudden, she was an avid equestrian. It was all he could do to keep from patting himself on the back.

Maggie insisted on leading her own horse down the aisle and out into the yard. Willing herself to be brave, she took hold of Killer's reins near the bit and started toward the wide opening at the far end of the long stable. The sound of steel-shod hooves ringing on the concrete made her stomach queasy. The animal ambling along beside her stood five feet three inches tall at the shoulder. She couldn't see over his back. Katie had once told her the average thoroughbred weighed around twelve hundred pounds. That was one thousand seventy pounds more than her own weight.

Winding their way around grooms mucking out stalls and stray dogs exploring their foster home, they exited the stable at the end that faced the outdoor arena. In the ring, Ry's trainer, Christian Atherton, was putting Rough Cut through his paces over an array of jumps. The big bay Hanoverian moved with power and grace, cantering to his fences lazily, then sailing over them with an ease that was positively arrogant.

Maggie watched, feeling a mixture of awe and fear. The handsome Atherton made it look easy. Maggie knew it was not. A fall on a difficult course had nearly killed Katie Quaid five years ago when she had been in contention for a spot on the Olympic show jumping team. Even after years of intense training, a masterful equestrian faced risks. Horses could be unpredictable.

She cast a dubious glance at Killer. The horse was half dozing, flipping his lips together, a habit that made him look as if he were talking to himself. She didn't want to imagine what he was saying—probably something about lulling a greenhorn into a false sense of security.

"Leg up?" Ry asked impatiently. He hadn't missed the way Maggie had been watching the horse and rider in the arena. Particularly the rider, he imagined. If there was a woman on the face of the earth who was immune to the cultured British charm of Christian Atherton, Ry had yet to meet her. Chris, while a close friend, was everything Ry was not—handsome, charming, sophisticated, worldly, the consummate ladies' man. None of that had bothered Ry before; he aspired to none of those things. Suddenly he was ready to bellow like a wounded moose because Maggie's gaze had lingered on the man a second longer than was necessary.

Too preoccupied to notice Ry's new mood, Maggie congratulated herself. She'd picked up a book on horsemanship the same day she had purchased her outrageously expensive riding clothes. The book had explained the rudiments of riding, step by step. "Leg up" was a term she was now thoroughly familiar with. She took the correct position beside the horse, lifting her left foot behind her so Ry could assist her in mounting.

"Your Mr. Atherton is one of the best, isn't he?" she asked innocently.

Ry's grumbled answer was lost in her squeal of surprise as he grabbed her ankle and nearly tossed her over the horse. She had to grab Killer around the neck to keep from landing in a water trough. As Ry mounted his horse, Maggie righted herself in the saddle and pushed her hair out of her eyes. She watched as Rough Cut started to refuse a fence, then took it in a tremendous leap that almost unseated his rider.

Working her reins into her gloved hands, Maggie swallowed hard. She already felt that her perch on the brown gelding's back was a precarious one. This must have been how Humpty Dumpty felt, she thought, trying to will herself to have good balance. If Killer had to step over anything higher than his shadow, she was going to end up on her head. Maybe she should have bought that velvet-covered riding helmet after all.

She cast a surreptitious glance at Rylan. The breeze tossed his dark hair. He wasn't wearing a helmet, but then he'd been riding practically since he could walk.

"This trail we're going on . . . it doesn't have any jumps on it, does it? I mean, I'm not really in the mood for that sort of thing today," she hastened to add.

His humor returning, Ry rubbed a hand across his mouth and shook his head. "No, no jumps." He nudged his mount with his heels and began leading the way out of the stable yard toward the wooded hills. Unable to resist, he glanced over his shoulder and said, "Just a little bit of water to swim through."

Maggie's stomach did a back flip. She turned her wide brown eyes on the animal beneath her. Killer didn't exactly resemble a sea horse. In fact, he looked distinctly *un*seaworthy. She urged him after his stablemate, almost bouncing off when he swung into a loose-limbed trot. "Uh, Rylan, sugar, can we discuss this swimming business?"

"Don't worry, Mary Margaret," Ry said straight-faced. "Horses are excellent swimmers—as long as their rider knows what he's doing."

Maggie gulped. *Lord have mercy, you're in trouble now, McSwain.*

What Maggie spent half the ride imagining as a raging torrent turned out to be a pretty little stream with a bed of pebbles. Not only did the horses not have to swim through it, they barely even noticed it as they waded through.

"Very amusing, Rylan," she remarked sardonically.

"I thought so," he said with a chuckle.

The ride was pleasant—generally. Killer turned out to be as amiable as Ry had promised, which helped Maggie relax somewhat. But she hadn't realized how quickly her uninitiated body would begin to protest the unfamiliar activity. She was no health nut, but she did get a certain amount of exercise in her work, running around for clients, going up and down the stairs of the homes she had to decorate. Lately she had also been on another of her sporadic workout kicks.

She discovered, however, that riding a horse exercised muscles nothing else did. Her ankles burned with pain from trying to maintain the correct position of heels down. Her arms and shoulders ached from trying to steer Killer away from the bushes he wanted to snack on. Her thighs began to quiver from gripping the saddle. Her new boots made her feet ache. Not even proper breeches could keep her bottom from getting saddle-sore.

Still, she enjoyed the ride when she wasn't biting back a groan of discomfort. The scenery was breath-taking. Wandering over the hills that were decked out in fall's blaze of color, she couldn't help thinking there wasn't a place on earth more beautiful than Virginia in autumn. If she could master sitting on a horse without fear of imminent death, she could picture spending many hours riding over these hills with Ry.

Damnation, he was handsome in black boots and skintight gray breeches that did nothing to disguise his muscular thighs or the impressive evidence of his gender. The black polo shirt he wore strained itself across his shoulders and chest. In another century he would have made a magnificent knight—powerful, back erect, hands light on the reins. Maggie would have gotten dizzy looking at him if she hadn't already been dizzy from sitting on top of a four-legged sky-scraper.

"That was your stallion your trainer was riding, wasn't it?" she asked, trying to get her mind off the flex and play of the muscles in his thighs.

"Yep, that was him. Rough Cut."

"Katie tells me you're going to retire him."

Ry's narrowed eyes watched her carefully. "His last competition is in two weeks—the Albemarle Cup Grand Prix. He gets a few months off, then starts standing at stud in February."

"Oh." Maybe this wasn't the greatest topic after all, Maggie thought. She wanted to show an interest in his business, but she really didn't think talking about studs and servicing and the like was going to do much to get her mind off Rylan's body.

Side by side their horses trudged up a short, steep hill, following an old logging trail that made a wide, clean path through the woods.

"If you retire your best horse, will Mr. Atherton stay on?"

Ry turned sharply in his saddle, his expression intense enough to bore through solid steel. "Why the hell would you care?"

Maggie was so startled, she nearly jumped off her horse. "I was just asking!"

"If you're so all-fire keen on Atherton, why don't you go riding with him? I'm sure he'd be more than happy to give you *private lessons,*" he said with a sneer.

"I'm not—I don't want—" she stammered,

completely taken aback by Ry's behavior. "What in the world's gotten into you? Did you get bit by one of those mountain ticks or something? You're raving like a lunatic. All I did was ask a simple question!"

"Gosh almighty." He swore long and fluently under his breath as much at his own behavior as anything. What was the matter with him all of a sudden?

"Well, is he?" Maggie asked.

"Is he what?" he snapped.

"Staying on as your trainer."

"Yes."

She rolled her eyes and heaved a long-suffering sigh. "Fine."

"Hmph," he said with a snort. "Sure it is."

Maggie stared at him speculatively, a slow smile curving her mouth. "Why, Rylan Quaid, I do believe you're jealous."

His scowl intensified. "Am not."

She grinned to herself. Point to McSwain. She was so happy, she nearly forgot she was on a horse and almost launched herself into Ry's arms. If he cared enough to get jealous, then she had something more to build on besides lust.

She batted her lashes at him coyly and conjured up her most seductive voice. "You don't have anything to worry about, sugar; he's not half the man you are."

Ry blushed burgundy. "Crimeny, Mary Margaret."

It was bad enough he kept catching glimpses of her breasts swaying seductively beneath her blouse. He sure didn't need her making suggestive remarks. He was ready to tackle her off her horse and have his way with her right there in the woods.

That would be the end of his plan. Maggie wanted someone charming and sophisticated, not a bull elk in rut. If he acted on his rampaging lust, he'd only be proving he was indeed too crude for an admiral's daughter.

When they emerged from the woods, Maggie was surprised to find they had looped around the farm and were now at the entrance gate. Horses in the fenced pastures raised their heads from grazing to look at them. A scruffy little brown-spotted dog sat by the gate post as if he had been waiting for them. Ry took one look at the animal and started scowling.

"Well, hell," he muttered.

"One of yours?" Maggie asked, pulling Killer to a halt beside Ry's horse.

"He is now."

Ry dismounted. Handing Maggie his reins, he approached the little mutt with his eye on the dog's wounded left front paw. The dog dropped its ears and whined pathetically as Ry squatted down in front of it. The animal was in terrible health, thin and dull-eyed. Ry shook his head. "You aren't nothing more than a scrap of hair and some bones, are you?"

"Do you think somebody left him off?" Maggie asked as she watched him carefully examine the dog's paw. She knew it wasn't at all unusual for people to leave unwanted pets at the end of the Quaid Farm driveway. One of the few things that was well known about Ry was that he never turned away an animal in need of his help. His farm buildings were populated with dogs and cats he had nursed back to health. He made an effort to find homes for the animals, but many ended up staying on. Katie had told her once his feed bill was horrendous.

"Hard to say. He's not wearing a collar, but he doesn't seem wild." Anger bumped his blood pressure up a notch. "Gosh almighty, people who don't take care of an animal any better than this ought to be strung up."

Maggie's heart ached with love at the gentle way Ry handled the frightened dog. He picked it up and carried it in the crook of one strong arm, talking to it in a soothing tone of voice. She was dead-on right about Rylan Quaid; there was a man full of tenderness under that cactus hide of his. If she was half as successful in bringing it out as this little dog was, she would consider her plan a major triumph.

She could see it now, playing out on the stage of her imagination: the look in his eyes as he realized she was the one person who could see the tenderness and sensitivity inside him. Their gazes would meet, silent understanding binding them together, soul to soul. Then he'd whisper her name and say—

"Y'all don't have a dog out at Poplar Grove, do you?" Ry shifted the terrier on his arm as they rode up the long tree-lined drive toward the stables.

"Hmm? What?" Maggie dragged her attention away from her dreams and pulled her gaze off the patchwork of pastures squared off by dark plank fences to focus on Ry.

"I said, I'm glad you volunteered to adopt this dog and take it home to Poplar Grove."

Maggie shook her head. "Oh, no, no, no. No dogs at Poplar Grove. Don't try to foist that little fleabag off on me, Rylan. I have Miss Emma and Mrs. Claiborne to consider."

"I bet they'd love a dog. Junior here is the perfect size for them."

"Rylan," she said sternly. Plan or no plan, she was going to have to put her foot down. "You cannot turn a dog loose in a house full of museum-quality antiques. Imagine the damage he could do."

Ry looked from the dog to Maggie. "I ask you, Mary Margaret, is this the face of a dog who would wreak havoc?"

Floppy ears perked up above woeful brown eyes as the dog gazed at Maggie. He had the potential to be adorable. It was impossible to say anything mean to his face.

"Must have taken acting lessons from Benji," she muttered.

"A *friend* would take this animal off my hands," Ry said with a meaningful lift of his dark eyebrows.

So he was going to play dirty, was he? Maggie's ripe little mouth pinched into an annoyed frown. Darn him, he'd outfoxed her. Now she was going to be stuck with that mangy mutt. "Not until he's had a flea bath and is in decent health, *friend.*" She ground the word between her teeth like grist in a mill. "The way he looks now, he'd scare off the tourists."

"I'll get him fixed up right as rain. Wouldn't have it any other way."

"Don't look so smug, sugar," she warned, taking one hand off the reins long enough to shake a finger at him and his self-satisfied smile. "You owe me for this, and I *will* collect."

"Collection time," she muttered to herself on a long, heartfelt groan as her numb feet hit the floor of the stable. She leaned heavily against Killer, her cheek pressed to the smooth leather of the saddle flap. Ry hadn't bothered to help her down off the horse, so she had managed the task herself, deciding it was probably a lot like rappelling down the side of a mountain.

The ride had barely ended and already she felt as if someone had flogged her from head to foot with the narrow edge of a yardstick. The silver lining to this black cloud of pain was the payment she planned to extract from Rylan: a long, slow rubdown by a pair of big, strong hands.

"You're a genius, Mary Margaret," she whispered to herself. But when she turned to tell Ry of her magnificent and wonderfully devious plan, he was preoccupied with the dog.

"Marlin will see to the horses," he said, leaving his mount with the groom. He turned and headed for the room where the medical supplies were kept, stepping around a three-legged black lab and over a beagle. The terrier was still slung over his arm and seemed to be enjoying the ride. His ears perked in interest as he panted happily.

Maggie followed, only temporarily thwarted by Rylan's disinterest. It took all her concentration to put one foot in front of the other. The muscles of her calves seemed elongated and uncontrollable. Her lower back was cramping, and her bottom hadn't been as sore since the time her daddy had spanked her for calling her sister Lisa Jane a poop-head during church. Wincing, she sank gratefully onto the nearest chair and watched while Ry collected the supplies he needed from the orderly, well-stocked medicine cabinet.

She watched him work with quiet efficiency, carefully cleaning the dog's wounded paw, applying medication and a neat white bandage, all the while mumbling to the dog affectionately. The little dog sat whimpering, but never tried to get away, obviously trusting Ry.

"You're very good at that," Maggie said.

He shrugged the compliment off. "It cuts down on my vet bill if I can handle minor problems myself."

His modesty touched a sweet spot in her heart. Katie had told her that Ry had never given up studying veterinary medicine, even though their father's death had prevented him from finishing his schooling. He obviously had a talent for it. She wondered if he ever wished things had worked out differently. Would he tell her if she asked? She doubted it. It was too soon. But he would open up to her eventually. She promised herself he would.

When he finished with the dog, Ry put the terrier in a roomy wire cage with food and water, then went to wash his hands at the utility sink. "He'll stay in there until we get him fed up a bit. That way he doesn't have to compete with the others at feeding time, and he won't run off his calories. I reckon he'll mostly eat and sleep for a few days anyway. I'll let you know when he's ready to go home with you."

"I can hardly wait," Maggie muttered. What had she gotten herself into? Miss Emma was flexible; she'd probably go for a dog. Mrs. Claiborne, on the other hand, was something of a starched skirt. At any rate, she didn't have to think about it for the moment.

"I'm starved," Ry announced. His stomach grumbled loudly to accent the statement. "Let's go up to the house and get something to eat."

"All right," Maggie said, but she didn't move.

Ry turned with his hand on the doorknob. "Come on, Mary Margaret, before I keel over from starvation."

It had probably been all of two hours since his last meal, she thought crossly. She looked up at him with a pained smile. "I'd love to, sugar. There's one minor problem, however."

"What's that?"

She gave a little shrug that set off explosions of pain in her shoulders. "I can't get out of this chair. My muscles are all frozen."

"Jeepers cripes." Rylan muttered under his breath. He moved to stand in front of Maggie, bent down, slid his hands under her arms, and lifted her off the chair.

Slowly she straightened out her cramped legs until her feet touched the floor. "Thank you."

"Don't mention it," Ry said, threads of hoarseness running through his voice. His palms were pressed against the sides of her full breasts. With a twist of the wrist he could have filled his hands with ripe, womanly softness. His mouth went dry. Lord, he wanted this woman. In another minute his desire was going to be obvious to anyone who glanced at the front of his breeches.

He forced himself to step back, trying to detach

himself physically and emotionally. He even managed to sound practical when he said, "When you get home, you'll have to give yourself a rubdown with good strong liniment."

"You've got it half right, darlin'," Maggie said, giving him a slow, devious smile. "I'm going to get a rubdown." She tapped a forefinger against his breastbone. "And *you're* going to give it to me."

Ry felt his stomach drop down to his knees. Immediately his mind conjured up images of black satin sheets and love lotions, candles burning and Maggie stretched out naked, waiting for his hands to glide over her creamy flesh.

"Me?" he asked weakly, barely able to hear himself for the blood roaring in his ears.

She glanced meaningfully from Rylan to the dog, then back to Rylan. "You owe me one, *friend.*"

"Lord, what is that awful smell?" Maggie asked, her face twisted into a grimace. She was stretched out on her belly across the white chenille spread on Ry's bed, a king-size blue towel wrapped around her.

She had insisted on a long, hot shower before her massage, thinking that would give Ry plenty of time to get himself worked up. She hadn't missed the desire in his eyes when they'd stood inches apart in the stable dispensary. He wanted her, she could see it. Why he was holding himself in check was beyond her, but his celibacy, where she was concerned, was at an end.

The plan was perfect. By the time he rubbed all the knots out of her muscles, she would be in the mood for love, and she would have full use of her body back. Ry would be aroused from running his hands over her naked skin. But the aroma wafting from the brown bottle Ry held told her there was one thing she hadn't foreseen.

"It's liniment," he said, biting the words off. Damn her, he thought, trying to fight the fire in his loins with anger. He looked furious, but there was something much warmer in his eyes as his gaze traveled down beyond her towel to her nicely rounded legs and dainty feet.

"It smells like the stuff you use on the horses."

"It is."

She lifted a delicately arched brow. "The same?"

"Diluted."

Maggie bit back a giggle. Ry didn't like the corner she had so neatly backed him into. The ornerier he got, the shorter his sentences, the darker his scowl. Ominous was a pale word for the look he was wearing now. *Well, tough,* she thought. She wasn't exactly pleased with his counterstrategy either, but if she had to make love with him smelling like a show jumper, then so be it.

Ry sat down on the bed with his back to Maggie, careful not to let his hip brush against her. When he leaned over to lift one of her feet, she rolled into him—and his hip wasn't the only thing she came in contact with.

"Dammit, Mary Margaret." He managed to speak with his jaw clenched.

Maggie gasped at the feel of his manhood, rock-solid, against her hip. A thrill of anticipation shot through her, settling low in her belly in a tight aching knot. She had to force the air back out of her lungs. "I can't help it if you sink the mattress like a ton of bricks."

Swearing under his breath, Ry scooted nearer the edge of the bed until he was darn near falling off. He poured a dollop of the foul-smelling liniment into his palm and began working on Maggie from the feet up, telling himself it wasn't any different from rubbing down one of his hunters.

The hell it wasn't.

His fingers worked over the arch of her foot, up to her ankle, and on to her shapely calf. Her skin was as soft as satin, warm to the touch. As his imagination told him what it would feel like to have her legs wrapped around him, the massage gradually changed from therapeutic to sensual. The movements of his hands slowed from vigorous rubbing to languid caressing.

Lord, it turned him on to see her stretched out on his bed! Heat poured over him in a shower of pinpricks down his back. What sweet heaven it would be to have her there every night, to take her in his arms, and spend hours loving her.

Loving her.

Denial and desire clashed inside him. Ry shook himself out of the fantasy. His fingers dug into the backs of her thighs.

"Ouch!" Maggie complained, tensing at the pain. "Will you watch it? That leg isn't going to win any prizes jumping fences, but I'm rather fond of it, myself."

"Sorry." He abandoned her thigh for her other foot, stalling. The longer it took him to get to her softer parts, the more in control he would be by the time he got there. At least that was what he tried to tell himself. He closed his eyes and tried to picture Maggie as a giant lump of bread dough— something without personality, without sex appeal.

Maggie began to relax as Ry's fingers worked magic on her stiff, sore muscles. Drowsy, she let her gaze wander the bedroom. It was a comfortable room furnished with lovely old cherrywood pieces. The walls were a soft blue, and the area rug covering part of the wood floor was deep royal blue. The grouping of prints on one wall was obviously Katie's work; Maggie recognized her partner's decorating touch instantly. Everything else within her range of vision was pure Rylan.

Basic male grooming tools were arranged neatly on his dresser. On the nightstand was a wine-glass, a horse magazine, and a dog-eared copy of

Ulysses. He was full of contradictions, her Rylan.

Her Rylan. That sounded almost as nice as his massage felt. She closed her eyes and sighed. Heavenly. Inch by inch he was relieving her pain. The tension was seeping out of her body, her muscles forgetting all about Killer as they relaxed. As Ry began slowly working his way up her thigh, she let herself picture what was going to happen later on.

Ry would start rubbing her shoulders, then she would turn over and he would loosen the towel. His stormy eyes would darken with desire, and he would lean over and kiss her. His hand would glide up over her hip, her waist, to her breast. She would help him out of his clothes, and he would stretch out on the bed with her and take her in his arms. His hard, muscular body would press her down into the mattress. It would happen the same way it did in the romance novels she read voraciously. It would be just the way she'd dreamed it a hundred and fifty thousand times. It would be, she sighed again . . . wonderful . . .

Ry shifted positions and stared down at Maggie. She lay with her arms stretched out wide, her face turned away from him. Her shoulders beckoned, bare, lovely. Beneath the thick blue terry towel she wore, her supple back awaited his touch. He knew without being able to see it that it tapered sharply to a tiny waist that flared into womanly hips. A hundred years ago someone would have painted a reclining nude of her and hung it above the bar in the local saloon. Maggie didn't have a fashionable figure, but it certainly appealed to him.

In fact, it was appealing to him more and more. He slid his palms along her shoulders and began kneading the tender flesh, remembering vividly the way her breasts had felt. He wanted to do more than remember. All he had to do was turn her over. He wanted to. He wanted to see her breasts, touch them, taste them. He wanted to know what color her nipples were, what size they were, how sensitive they were.

He wanted her, period. She wanted him too. A man didn't miss the kind of signals Maggie had been sending out. He was denying them both because he thought he wouldn't be able to hold himself back once he touched her. That was probably ridiculous. The rationalization began in his head, growing louder in direct proportion to the intensity of the ache in his lower body.

It wasn't as if he were a randy teenager. He was a grown man, an experienced man. Certainly he would be able to shut out the fact that just looking at Maggie turned him half wild.

He slid one hand down her back to the bottom edge of the towel and slipped it beneath, groaning deep in his throat at the feel of her soft, rounded bottom.

"Maggie," he whispered, bending over her. His lips brushed the shell of her ear, the scent of shampoo penetrating the scent of the liniment he'd rubbed into her muscles. "Maggie."

He expected her to roll toward him, a feline smile gracing her mouth as she lifted the lids on those magnificent brown eyes of hers. Maybe she would open the towel herself, or watch while he did, then put her arms around him and pull him down.

She didn't move an inch.

He murmured her name again, anticipation pulling his nerves as tight as a bowstring. Was she nervous? Maybe she was having second thoughts. Maybe she'd decided she couldn't make love with a big idiot farmer who had rubbed horse liniment over her when the situation had clearly called for something exotic like passion-fruit oil.

Ry stared down at her for a long moment. His senses honed razor sharp by sexual tension, he was acutely aware of the different shades of red in her glossy, tousled hair, of the feel of her skin beneath his fingertips, of the soft, unmistakable sound of her snoring.

Snoring?

Ry leaned over further to get a good look at her face. Dark lashes curved against her cheek. Her soft lips were slightly parted. She was sound asleep. The horseback ride had exhausted her, and the massage had relaxed her. He'd finally decided to make love to her, and she was unconscious.

"Well, hell."

four

"WHAT ON EARTH is that awful smell?" Mrs. Claiborne sat at the head of the dining table, her fork hovering over a plate of scrambled eggs, her slim nose wrinkled in distaste. She brought her other hand up to smooth the lace collar of her dress, as if the odor might somehow disturb the delicate fabric.

Maggie stopped in the act of pulling a chair back from the table. The half bottle of perfume had obviously been a wasted effort. Now she simultaneously cursed Rylan Quaid and scanned her brain for an answer to Mrs. Claiborne's question that would gracefully and quickly put an end to the subject.

Across the table, Miss Emma, dressed in a pink sweat suit, her fine hair mussed around her head, sniffed the air like an eager foxhound, mischief gleaming in her eyes. "Smells like a touch of Passion's Promise over horse liniment. What's the story on this, McSwain?" A naughty smile tipped up her lips as her delicately lined face lit up with the glow of anticipation. "Is it kinky?"

Maggie ground her teeth. Her hand tightened visibly on the back of her chair. "No, it's not kinky. In fact, it's not at all worth discussing."

"You can tell us, Mary Margaret," Miss Emma

assured her in a conspiratorial tone as she tore a biscuit in two and baptized half in a puddle of raspberry jam. "We've been around the block a time or two, you know."

Mrs. Claiborne sniffed. "A time or two? You darn near ran your tires bald."

Miss Emma's answer was an impish grin.

Maggie took her seat, snapping open a linen napkin as if it were a bullwhip. "There's nothing to tell."

She had awakened the previous afternoon on Rylan's bed—alone, untouched, frustrated, and furious with herself. How many years had she been waiting for Rylan Quaid to make love to her, only to fall asleep when the perfect opportunity presented itself!

He certainly had been ready if not willing. She almost groaned aloud at the memory of the accidental intimate contact they made when he sat down on the bed. At least there was one part of him that was living up to her dreams. And she had zonked out. Her big seduction scene and she had nodded off before they'd even gotten to the good part.

Of course, the scene might have been salvaged had Ry come into the room to awaken her. He could have stretched out beside her and wooed her out of sleep with a string of soft kisses that started at her temple and trailed downward over her cheek to just under her jaw to the hollow at the base of her throat. She would have sighed, half awake, watching him through lowered lashes as he tugged the towel away from her breasts to capture an aroused peak in his mouth. . . .

Instead, he'd bellowed through the door that he had a hunt club meeting in thirty minutes, and she'd better quit sawing logs and haul her tail out of bed. The rude, overbearing, overgrown ox. What kind of gentleman insinuated that a lady snored?

Damnation. Her clever plan had gotten her nowhere, and nothing on God's green earth could scrub the scent of that blasted horse liniment off her skin. She'd soaked in a tub slick with a double dose of rose-scented bath oil and gotten nothing but slippery. She'd fumigated her room with a cloud of Passion's Promise, but she still smelled like Mr. Ed.

"I knew a French chef once," Miss Emma said dreamily. Gazing at the brass chandelier, she pressed a frail-looking hand to her heart as if feeling it beat would somehow sharpen her age-dimmed memory. "We met at a little sidewalk café in Antwerp, Belgium. He used to do the most delicious things with olive oil. I declare, it makes my heart race to think of it."

"It ought to make your nose grow," Mrs. Claiborne said with a snort as she cut a bite from her slice of ham. "You've never been to Belgium. You've never been farther than Biloxi."

Miss Emma gave her sister a peeved look. "So I

77

got the location mixed up. Sue me. It must have been New Orleans and it just seemed like Antwerp." She turned back to Maggie with the sincere look of a schoolteacher at lesson time. "The point is, different men find different things erotic. With André it was olive oil. Baron Huntleigh once went wild watching me eat a fig. If Rylan finds horse liniment stimulating, darlin'—"

"Believe me, Miss Emma," Maggie cut her off as she mutilated a slice of toast with a butter knife. "Rylan doesn't find horse liniment stimulating. I'm sure I haven't the first idea what Rylan Quaid finds erotic."

Miss Emma looked puzzled. "Hadn't you better find out?"

Maggie intended to redouble her efforts to find out. She was going to crack that steely control of Ry's if it killed her. When she got through with him, he wouldn't be able to spell "just friends." However, she had no intention of discussing her plans with the ladies. She considered it something of a failure that Ry hadn't become a slave to her charms already, and she was no more willing to concede defeat than the rest of Dixie.

She sat back in her chair and took a casual sip of steaming coffee. "Have you ladies ever considered what fun it would be to own a dog?"

"I take it the honeymoon isn't over," Maggie drawled as she walked into Primarily Paper through the stockroom. She and Katie used the wallpaper and custom drapery store as a base for their decorating service. Her business partner was deeply involved in kissing her husband good-bye for the morning.

Nick raised his head and winked at Maggie. "What can I say? She can't get enough of me."

That sounded entirely possibly to the ears of someone who wasn't getting any from anyone, Maggie thought sourly.

Katie gazed up at Nick with stars in her eyes and a disgustingly happy pink glow on her cheeks. Her voice was seductively smoky when she spoke. "Can we discuss that statement in depth later?"

The look Nick gave his petite wife could have set the Arctic Ocean boiling. "At lunch." He dropped a quick kiss on her nose and turned to leave. "Bye, kitten. See ya, Maggie." He walked out whistling, pausing at the front door to flip the "Closed" sign to "Open."

"It's nice to see *some* of us are happy," Maggie said, dropping into the chair behind her desk. Too agitated to do any real work, she opened a file and pretended to search for the invoice on a shipment of wallpaper.

Katie turned toward her and started to make a retort, but stopped herself and sniffed the air instead. Her face pinched into a frown. "What in the world is that awful smell? It smells like"—she sniffed again—"horse liniment."

"Can we change the subject? How was Williamsburg? Are the leaves down there turned yet?" Maggie rattled on as if her partner were actually carrying on a conversation with her instead of circling her desk like a buzzard.

"No. Beautiful. Yes." Katie stopped in front of the desk, crossed her arms over her chest, and gave Maggie one of her patented no-nonsense looks. "Mary Margaret McSwain, would you kindly explain to me why you smell like Man O'War?"

Maggie was saved from having to answer by the jingle of the bells above the door. Rylan ambled in. Maggie's heart picked up a beat. Even though she was furious with him, she couldn't help but appreciate the way he looked in a pair of faded jeans or the way his powerful upper body filled out the navy blue T-shirt he wore. Lord, how she wanted to get her hands on that body of his!

Pulling his battered blue baseball cap off and combing his hair back with his fingers, Ry stepped around behind the counter. He went to his sister and bent to give her a peck on the cheek. "Welcome home, princess. That Yankee treatin' you decent?"

Katie gave him a saucy grin. "What if he isn't?"

"I'll take him apart, pack him in a crate, and ship him back to New Jersey." Ry's reply was calmly delivered, but there was an unmistakable glint of promise in his steely gaze. He was fiercely protective of Katie, not only as her big brother, but as her surrogate father as well. Katie had been only sixteen at the time of her father's death. Ry had considered himself her guardian from that day until the day she'd married Nick Leone.

"Over my dead body!" Katie giggled and hugged him around his hard waist. "What brings you down from your mountain?"

"Besides welcoming you home, I needed to pick up some vet supplies and dog food." Watching Maggie from the corner of his eye, he added as a deliberate afterthought, "Oh, and I came to talk to Maggie."

So she ranked somewhere below kibble on his list, did she? Maggie had to bite her tongue to keep from cutting him to ribbons with the remarks that sprang to mind.

He wasn't likely to fall in love with her if she jumped down his throat every time he made a careless remark, was he? If he was, as she suspected, wary of getting his heart involved, it wouldn't help her cause any to run him into the ground for such a minor injustice—no matter how furious it made her. Hadn't she told herself she had to be understanding, that it was going to take some work to bring out Ry's tender side? Of course she had. So she tamped her temper down, telling herself she would find an infinitely more pleasurable way to exact her revenge.

Ry watched the process of her rapid mood

change with amusement. Maggie was his match all right. Her mind was never still for an instant. They'd keep each other on their toes for the next forty or fifty years—once he got her to the altar.

She eased up out of her chair to perch on the edge of her desk, crossing her legs in a way that made her snug beige skirt ride up to her knees. "Why, Rylan, how sweet of you to drop by to see me." Leaning toward him, she presented her cheek to him as if she expected to be kissed, and batted her lashes.

"Got something in your eye, Mary Margaret?" He congratulated himself on keeping his own eyes off the way her bosom rose and fell beneath her soft brown sweater.

Maggie looked away from him and held her breath as she counted to ten. When she turned back, she wore a smile as brittle as an oak leaf in November. "No, darlin', but how considerate of you to ask. Just what did you want to speak to me about?"

"I'm bringing your dog over Saturday morning."

Maggie's jaw dropped. "You can't! You promised you'd keep him!"

"Until he was fit to leave. He'll be fit to leave by Saturday."

She slid off the desk and began pacing. "How can you know that? How can you know he won't have a relapse or something?"

Ry scowled at her. "If he has a relapse of

starvation, I'll take it out on your hide, Mary Margaret. You told me you'd take that dog and take care of him."

Her frown matched his. "You conned me into it. I haven't had enough time to talk it over with Miss Emma and Mrs. Claiborne yet. They're not entirely convinced it would be a good idea to have a dog at Poplar Grove." And if Mrs. Claiborne's reaction this morning had been any indication of how long it would be before a dog would reside at Poplar Grove, they had a long wait ahead of them. Maggie didn't think hell was liable to freeze over by the weekend. "Why can't you keep him another week?" *Or two or ten,* she wanted to add.

"Because someone dropped off a golden retriever this morning, and she's no more than a week away from having puppies. I need the space *your* dog is taking up, *friend,*" he said with a pointed look.

Maggie turned to her partner. Katie was trying to appear immersed in work, jotting notes as she went over some sketches of a house they were working on. Maggie mustered up her sweetest, most appealing smile. "Katie, darlin', wouldn't your dog just love to have a playmate?"

"Sure he would," she said dryly. "But then where would Nick and I live? Our house isn't big enough for my wolfhound to have playmates."

"Damnation," Maggie muttered under her breath. She wheeled hopefully as the front door opened and another friendly face came into view. "Zoe, sugar, wouldn't your kids love to have a dog, a sweet, little, adorable dog? Why, he's no bigger than a toy."

Zoe Baylor smoothed the skirt of her nurse's uniform as she took a seat at the table where sample books of wallpaper were piled. "Girl, our sweet little adorable cat who isn't any bigger than a toy had kittens on my new sofa yesterday. The last thing I need is to throw a dog into the bargain."

"Face it, friend," Ry said smugly. "Junior is your dog, and he's coming to live with you."

Maggie leaned a hip against her desk and ground her teeth, having no trouble whatsoever dreaming up methods of revenge.

Ry reached out and tweaked her cheek. "By the way, get out your party dress. We're going to a dinner sponsored by the Virginia Grand Prix Association a week from Friday night." He turned to leave, then stopped and turned back, sniffing the air with a devilish sparkle in his eye. "That a new perfume you're wearing, Mary Margaret?"

She couldn't speak for a full thirty seconds after he left. It took that long to wrestle back the urge to run after him and bean him with her paperweight. Finally she glanced at Zoe and Katie and said, "Sweeps a girl right off her feet, doesn't he?"

The look on Katie's face mixed bewilderment and amusement. "What was that all about?"

"Here's the *Reader's Digest* version: Rylan proposed to me because he thought it was the practical thing to do, then he took it back and suggested we be 'just friends.'"

"Rylan *proposed* to you?" Katie's gray eyes went moon-round.

Maggie frowned. "He doesn't love me, Katie."

"Did he say that?" Zoe asked gently.

"He didn't have to." She sank back against the edge of her desk, her shoulders slumping dejectedly. "He ran down his checklist of reasons why we should get married; love wasn't one of them."

"So are you 'just friends'?"

Maggie's gaze burned through the plate glass window as she stared at Ry across the street where he stood talking with Katie's husband. "Yeah. Like Lee and Grant." She turned back to her best friend of nearly ten years with her heart in her eyes. "I love him, Katie. I want him to be my husband, but I won't marry a man who doesn't love me."

"He's had some rough breaks, Maggie. Be patient with him," Katie pleaded for her brother's sake.

"You mean because of your mother leaving?" Maggie asked, needing to hear her own theory proved right.

"Partly. Ry grew up not trusting women. Then something happened when he was at college. I know he was serious about a girl there, then he had to come home when Daddy died, and he never mentioned her again. I tried to find out what happened, but you know Ry. Getting a story out of him is like trying to pull a grizzly bear's teeth. I finally gave up. He's spent a long time nursing old wounds and protecting himself from new ones, Mag. Those kind of walls are hard to break down. I ought to know; Nick had to scale a bunch of them to get to me."

Yes, Maggie thought, the walls Ry had built and fortified around his heart would be difficult to tear apart, but she was determined to do it. There was a man behind those walls who needed love and who had love to give, whether he realized it or not. She knew he did. In her heart, in her dreams, she *knew*.

"I can handle it," she said, tapping a finger to her lips as the wheels started turning in her head.

A fond smile split Zoe's thin dark face. "I recognize that scheming look, Maggie. What are you planning?"

A slow, self-satisfied smile turned up the corners of Maggie's lips. "When the going gets tough, the tough go shopping. I'm going to drive up to D.C. and buy myself a dress for that party next week. A dress hot enough to melt granite. Then Lord have mercy on that big ornery brother of yours, Katie, 'cause I've set my sights on him, and I mean to have him." Her smile broke into a full-fledged grin that glowed with mischief as she winked at Katie. "You know what they say, darlin': All's fair in love and war."

Katie chuckled. "Which one is this?"

"A little bit of both, sugar. A little bit of both."

The first herd of tourists had already descended on Poplar Grove when Ry pulled into the yard in his pickup. Cars from five different states and one province of Canada were lined up in the parking area. A group of about fifteen people stood on the lawn in front of the manor, their attention focused on Mrs. Claiborne as she spoke and gestured at the white columns and up to the carved pineapple finial that crowned her home.

Ry glanced at the little spotted dog curled up on the seat beside him. "You're home, Junior. I sure hope you like crowds."

He was about to reach for the door handle, when he spotted Maggie hurrying across the forecourt. She was a vision out of the colonial past dressed in a long dark blue gown with a tightly fitted waist. Frothy lace trimmed the snug sleeves and edged the deeply cut square neckline.

Ry sat back and groaned in dismay. How men ever walked around in skintight breeches back then was beyond him, what with all the women running around in dresses that displayed a lady's charms to such perfection. To make matters worse, Maggie was wearing a pendant that swayed and bobbed just above her breasts and drew his gaze downward. As if her cleavage wasn't enough on its own.

She swung the passenger door open and climbed up into the truck with a wicker picnic basket. When she closed the door, the cab was immediately filled with the pungent scent of Passion's Promise.

"Jeepers cripes, Mary Margaret," Ry said, coughing. "That perfume's enough to choke a horse!"

Maggie scowled at him. Somehow her hot shower had only served to make matters worse. Apparently it had opened her pores and let the perfume soak in. "Please, Rylan, all this flattery will make me light-headed."

"That's not the flattery making you light-headed, you're being overcome by fumes."

A minor detail only a mannerless swine would call attention to. She must be bonkers to love a man with so little couth, Maggie thought. But love him she did. A tired smile lifted the corners of her mouth. "I had a little accident this morning. At least I don't smell ready to run for the roses anymore."

"What are you doing in that getup?" Ry asked, fighting to keep his eyes off her breasts.

"One of the tour guides called in sick today. I'm taking her place."

She glanced at the little dog curled up next to

Rylan's thigh and frowned again. It hardly looked like the same animal they had found wounded and abandoned only a matter of days ago. He'd been bathed and fed. His coat was now snow white with mahogany-colored spots. He wore a collar with a rabies vaccination tag affixed to it. His injured paw was wrapped in a fresh bandage. Staring at her with shiny eyes, he perked his triangular ears up and barked at her. Maggie shook her head. Ry had worked a miracle with his skill and caring.

"We've got exactly fifteen minutes to sneak Junior here into the house," she said. "So here's the plan—"

"Sneak? What do you mean, sneak?"

"Well . . . I've discussed this at length with the ladies, and Mrs. Claiborne isn't convinced now would be the right time for us to take a dog on at Poplar Grove," Maggie explained diplomatically.

"When does she think the right time would be?"

"Oh . . . she said something about electing a red-eyed communist from Mars president first." She shook a finger at him. "See the trouble you're getting me into, friend? I'm liable to get thrown out of my home."

Then she could come and live with him, Ry thought, liking the idea a lot. He eyed the picnic basket. "What's that for? As if I couldn't guess."

"Miss Emma thinks Mrs. Claiborne would come around on the dog issue if she didn't see the dog until he was in the house already, fitting in with the surroundings. But if she catches us trying to take a dog into the house, she's liable to take a switch to the pair of us."

"So you've got Miss Emma in on the conspiracy."

"In on it? Sugar, it was her idea! She has a naturally devious mind," she said with more than a little admiration. A twinkle came into her sable eyes at Ry's look. He refused to believe little old ladies could think of anything but knitting and church. "Watch your back when you're around her, sugar. She pinched a man the other day."

"She what?"

"Pinched him. She said he had great buns, so she pinched him right on the—"

Ry scowled at her. "You're making that up."

"Am not, but we don't have time to argue about it now. Let's get a move on, Quaid."

Mrs. Claiborne's tour group had moved into the house by the time Ry and Maggie made it to the front porch. Ry carried the picnic basket with Junior's wet nose poking out from under the lid. Miss Emma was on the porch, starting her tour off with a liberally embroidered history of the plantation. Maggie often wondered how many of Miss Emma's fibs were pure mischief as opposed to poor memory. Quite a few, she suspected, if the sparkle in the old woman's eyes was anything to go by.

They stepped into the hall just as Mrs. Claiborne

and her group emerged from the dining room. Maggie swore under her breath. In another minute, she and Ry could have been up the stairs and home free. Now they would have to stop and chat as the guests browsed.

"Why, Mr. Quaid, what a pleasure!" Mrs. Claiborne smiled, crossing the room with a swish of her skirt and petticoats.

"Mornin', Miz Claiborne." Ry ducked his head, shifting the picnic basket to his other hand.

She glanced at the basket. "It's a lovely day for a picnic."

"Yes, ma'am."

"Where are you going?"

"Umm . . ." Feeling as if he were ten all over again and lying to Miss Thornbrush about cutting Sunday school, he shot a desperate glance at Maggie, who leaned toward her landlady with a concerned look.

"Miss Emma is telling that story about being abducted off the veranda by a British colonel in her previous life again."

Mrs. Claiborne rolled her eyes. "Excuse me, Mr. Quaid."

"Ma'am." He nodded, then heaved a sigh of relief.

"Quick," Maggie whispered, giving him a shove that didn't budge him an inch, "get upstairs before she comes back."

"Excuse me, miss?"

Maggie ground her teeth as she turned to face a balding bespectacled tourist with a nasal New York accent. Reminding herself about Southern hospitality, she plastered a smile on her face. "Yes? How can I help you?"

"Can you explain to me about the cut-glass lids on these liquor decanters in the dining room? I didn't quite get that business about the shapes and the kinds of booze and all that."

"Certainly." Maggie followed the man back toward the dining room, sending Ry a look over her shoulder.

He turned to go upstairs but was confronted by a couple wanting to have their picture taken at the foot of the carved walnut staircase. He set the basket down to snap the photo, then all hell broke loose. A crash sounded in the parlor, followed by angry barking and a shout for help.

Maggie, Ry, and Mrs. Claiborne all made it to the parlor at the same time, followed by Miss Emma and the tourists. Perched on a drop-leaf table was one member of Mrs. Claiborne's tour group. Snarling up at the man was Junior. Ry squeezed his eyes shut. Maggie pressed a hand to her mouth. Miss Emma covered her ears. Mrs. Claiborne glared accusingly at the three of them.

"Hey, will somebody call this mutt off?" the guy on the table demanded.

Ry stepped ahead and scooped up the dog with one big hand. "Sorry."

"Sorry? Huh! Sorry's not going to cut it, pal." The man slid to his feet, straightening his jacket and reaching up to comb his black hair into place with his fingers. One hand inched back to the table for his camera bag while he maintained a furious expression. "I oughta sue."

"Mr. Quaid," Mrs. Claiborne said sternly, her gaze directed at Ry, then Junior, "did you bring this animal into this house?"

Ry swallowed hard. "Yes, ma'am."

Maggie's eyes suddenly went wide. "And it's a good thing he did," she said, stepping forward. Glaring at the tourist, she snatched away a polished pewter candlestick that was poking up out of his camera bag. "Would you care to explain how this came to be in your possession, sir?"

Mrs. Claiborne's hand went to her heart. "The Revere candlestick! That's been in this family for over two hundred years!"

The thief flung his camera bag at them and bolted for the back door. Ry shoved Junior into Mrs. Claiborne's arms and charged after the man, who made it to the bottom of the steps before Ry flew off the porch and tackled him. The thief was sandwiched between the ground and two hundred sixty-five pounds of solid muscle. Ry sat up, digging a knee into the man's back, and lifted the thief's head by a handful of hair. The culprit spit out a mouthful of grass and dirt and shot a glare over his shoulder at his captor.

Ry gave him a nasty smile. "You're in a world of hurt, slick."

Behind them, people came spilling out of the house. Maggie and Mrs. Claiborne hurried down the steps, Mrs. Claiborne clutching Junior to her breast.

"Oh, Mr. Quaid, you caught him. Thank heaven!"

"And I caught this one, sister!" Miss Emma called.

The crowd on the porch parted like the Red Sea as Emma marched a second rascal through the double doors at sword point. Maggie gasped as she recognized the man as the one who had lured her into the dining room on the excuse of gathering information about antique bottles.

"This coward thought he'd make a getaway while y'all were after his partner," Miss Emma said, swirling the tip of the sword under the man's nose. She was a peculiar sight—a tiny old lady in a colonial dress and high-top sneakers, wielding a relic from the War Between the States. "Granddaddy's pigsticker and I have persuaded him to stay until the police arrive."

"My hero," Maggie said with an impish grin and a melodramatic sigh. She clutched Ry's arm and leaned into him, bosom first. They stood in the yard, watching as the police car drove away bearing the would-be thieves.

Ry looked down at her, his eyes instantly drawn to the creamy globes straining the confines of her costume. Heat rose from his groin all the way to the tips of his ears. He tore his gaze away and fixed it on the crowd that was filing back to the house.

"Me the hero? Shoot. What about Miss Emma? I swear, I never saw anything like that. I thought she was gonna lop that guy's head off."

"Isn't she something? I keep telling you, sugar. Miss Emma is full of surprises. And you keep thinking all old ladies are interested in is drinking prune juice and tatting doilies." She shook her head in reproach as she stepped back from him. "We are going to have to do some serious work on your mistaken impressions about women."

Ry looked away, his expression dropping into his characteristic scowl. His impressions of women had been based on experience—bad experience. With the exception of his sister, the women he'd trusted had betrayed him. Maggie had her work cut out if she thought she could erase those harsh lessons from his memory.

"I think it's safe to say Junior has a home here now," she said.

"Aren't you glad I let you have the little guy?" Ry asked, letting go of his dark thoughts as Maggie led him by the hand into the old laundry building.

Maggie laughed. "*Let* me have? Ha! You'd

better thank your lucky stars that man was a thief, friend. You should've seen the look on your face when Mrs. Claiborne asked if you were the one who brought that dog in the house!"

"My face?" Ry laughed. "How about yours? I thought you were gonna lose your breakfast when you saw that guy sitting on the table with Junior yapping at his heels!"

They laughed until Maggie had tears rolling down her cheeks and Ry was holding his stomach. When they finally stopped to catch their breath, Ry leaned back against a work table piled with antique linens and shook his head in wonder. He hadn't laughed so much with a woman since . . . ever.

He hadn't given it much thought when he'd hatched his "just friends" scheme, but Maggie really was his friend. He liked her as a person and enjoyed her company; they could plot together and laugh together. Suddenly the idea of spending the rest of his life with her took on a whole new dimension, one he wasn't entirely sure he should trust.

Maggie wiped the last of her tears away and looked up at Ry, her heart tripping over the expression in his eyes. It was speculative, a little wary, and yet there was a vulnerability in it that made her want to take him in her arms. The moment caught and held.

Forgetting his own warning to keep his hands

off her, Ry reached up and touched her cheek, marveling at how soft she was beneath his calloused fingertips. He lowered his head and brushed his mouth across hers. His heart slammed into his ribs as her hands framed his face and drew him back for another, deeper kiss. Lord, she tasted sweet. And she smelled . . . like a quart of Passion's Promise.

The scent caught in his throat so that he had to draw back from her, coughing. "Maybe you ought to think about giving up perfume altogether, Mary Margaret."

five

IT WAS A dress so hot it could have sent Antarctica up in flames. Deep teal in color, the shimmering fabric clung to every strategic curve on her body. It seemed almost like a living thing, sliding over her as she walked, teasing the viewer as she wandered through the crowded ballroom making idle conversation. Strapless, the sequined bodice was heart-shaped, rounding over each breast and nipping in at her tiny waist. The sequins trailed down over her tummy in a suggestive arrow.

It was so tight, she looked as if she had been poured into it. Her breasts swelled temptingly above the edge of the gown, capturing the attention of the males present. They seemed to hold their breath in anticipation as the gown shifted with her every movement. The floor-length skirt was glove-snug and would have been restrictive if it hadn't been for the slit that exposed her right leg to midthigh. In a room full of tuxedos and evening gowns, she stood out like an emerald in a handful of lesser jewels.

No man with a hormone in his body could have looked at her and remained indifferent. So it had cost her a small fortune. Maggie considered it as necessary to her as the Pentagon budget was to the country. She had a battle of sorts to fight, and she meant to be armed to the teeth. Miss Emma had told her different men found different things erotic. She was going to try every one of them until Ry tossed her over his shoulder and carried her home. She was mounting a feminine offensive on all fronts, and she was determined to keep up the fight until Rylan surrendered himself to her love.

Tonight her role was seductress. She was playing it to the hilt.

"Do you think your horse is going to end his career on a high note tomorrow, Ry?" asked Clifton Brachman. He was one of the horse owners in the crowd, which included trainers and dignitaries from the international show world as well as the Virginia horse community.

Ry swore under his breath as he caught another male gaze lingering on Maggie's derriere. His hand tightened on the stem of his empty wine-glass until it quietly snapped and dropped to the rich red carpet. He kicked it under a table. The rest of the glass was angrily shoved into the hand of a passing waiter. He snatched up a fresh drink and tossed the contents back with none of his usual respect for good wine.

The man attempting to have a conversation with him backed away with a nervous smile. "G-good luck t-tomorrow."

Ry never heard a word he said. Maggie paused in her conversation with Katie and another woman to glance up at him and send him a smile brimming with seductive promise.

Another glass bit the dust.

Damn her. When he'd planned to lure her by pretending indifference, he hadn't counted on her reacting quite so enthusiastically. It was one thing to have her batting her eyelashes at him, but this dress was something else again. His plan was working, but damned if she wasn't wreaking havoc on his control!

He had held off making love to her for too long. That was the whole problem. He should have bedded her weeks ago and gotten this lust out of his system, instead of letting it simmer until it felt as though his blood was boiling in his veins.

His plan had been to end their wait after the party. He'd spent the week working like a dog, all the while telling himself over and over that he could hold his passion in check, that he could be patient and gentle with Maggie, that he could be careful with her and not rush her or hurt her.

All she'd had to do was show up in that dress, and his theory had been shot to hell. His control had gone up in smoke the second he'd set eyes on her. Then she'd insisted on sitting right beside him in the car so that his arm brushed against her every time he moved the steering wheel. It was a wonder he hadn't driven into a tree or something. Now he'd had to endure an hour of watching her slink around in the mouthwatering slip of silk and sequins, shimmering like a heat wave in the dog days of August.

He was ready to drag her into the nearest dark room and ravish her. If he looked at her for more than thirty seconds, he started getting hard. More than once since the evening began he'd had to shift positions in an attempt to hide his discomfort. It was all Maggie's fault.

And he was ready to kill the next man who came near her, glanced at her, or commented on her.

"Maggie looks good enough to be put on the dessert table this evening," a cultured British voice announced beside him.

Red-faced, fists knotted at his sides, Ry wheeled on his trainer.

Christian Atherton took a prudent step backward, but his lean, handsome face was bright with amusement, his pale blue eyes glittering. "Now see here, old boy, I was merely paying the lady a compliment! Touchy, aren't we?"

Ry grumbled under his breath about the British sense of humor.

After brushing back a lock of pale blond hair, Christian slipped his hands into the pockets of his formal black trousers and rocked back on his heels. "Don't worry, I won't stray into your territory. Pity the fool who does." He shot a speculative glance in Maggie's direction. "Carter Hill, for instance."

A growl actually rumbled low in Ry's throat as he leveled his gaze on Maggie and the corporate lawyer from an old-money family. The Hills were upstanding members of the Briarwood community and owned a small stable of hunters that competed well locally but not on a national or international scale. Carter Hill had dated Maggie in the past. It looked as though he was approaching her with interest in renewing the relationship.

And she was flirting with him, damn her pretty hide! Never mind that she'd been born flirtatious, that she seldom meant anything by it. She'd probably batted her long dark lashes at the doctor who'd delivered her. The point was, she was turning her charms toward a bona fide gentleman who came from a long line of bona fide gentlemen. It hit Ry in a spot that had been rubbed raw years ago. He wasn't a gentleman.

He glanced down at the tuxedo jacket he'd squeezed himself into. Who was he trying to fool?

Muttering swear words, he picked a fleck of lint off his lapel then ran a thick finger inside the starched wing collar of his shirt, swallowing uncomfortably. "Damn suit. I feel like a mule in horse harness."

"On the contrary," Christian said diplomatically. "You look very dapper." A mischievous grin spread across his mouth. "Didn't Maggie tell you so?"

Maggie had told him that the sight of a big strappin' man in a tuxedo made her heart flutter in her breast. With that wicked teasing look of hers, she'd invited him to feel for himself. He'd nearly busted the fly on his trousers just thinking about it. But now she was smiling at Carter Hill.

"She's asked me to give her riding lessons," Christian said.

And she was going to be spending time alone with the fourth son of the Earl of Westly, notorious playboy of the show-jumping world. Ry glared at his friend.

"Isn't that sweet?" Christian asked, the picture of innocence.

"You think that's *sweet?*" Ry ground the word like gravel under his boot heel.

"Oh, rather. She told me she wants to learn to ride to please you, that she wants to be able to spend more time with you on the farm. It's doubly sweet because she confessed to me she's terrified of horses, and she wasn't just saying that to be coy."

Ry stared down at his shoes, feeling like a heel. Here he was suspecting Maggie had designs on his trainer, when all she wanted was to please him. He knew she was afraid of horses, but she was willing to try to overcome that fear so she could spend more time with him. It really was sweet.

The thought made him uncomfortable. He could handle Maggie's being feisty. He could handle her scheming. But sweetness scared the living hell out of him. What was he supposed to do with sweetness? He couldn't return it; there wasn't anything sweet about him. And he didn't want to accept it, though he wouldn't admit why even to himself.

"See here," Christian said with a note of censure in his smooth voice, "you'll have to learn to curb that jealous temper of yours."

"I'm not jealous," Ry said, knowing it was a bald-faced lie.

Christian laughed as he swept a glass of champagne from the tray of a passing waiter. "Next you'll try to tell me you're not in love with her."

Ry looked at him sharply, his heartbeat picking up the extra stroke of panic. "I'm not in love with her. I like Maggie. I'm attracted to her. I think we could have a solid marriage."

"You're possessive of her and insanely jealous if another man so much as glances at her from across the room." Christian pressed a hand to Ry's broad shoulder and gave him a sympathetic look. "My dear friend, you need a lesson in romantic math. All those things add up to love."

He couldn't be in love with her, Ry told himself. He had promised himself a long time ago that he wouldn't fall into that trap again. He wanted to be partners with Maggie—in bed and out—but he couldn't give her his heart. He wasn't capable of it anymore. Besides, it didn't make good sense for a man like him to give his heart to a woman. She would only give it back. He had good qualities: He was loyal, he would be faithful, he was a hard worker, a good provider. Those were fine qualities, but they weren't the things that inspired women to write love sonnets.

His eyes found Carter Hill again, and he wished the poor man to the blackest corner of hell simply because he looked perfectly at ease in a tuxedo. Well, a tuxedo was the next to the last thing Ry needed. The last was to fall in love. Fortifying the walls he'd built around his heart, he told himself yet again that he would have Maggie McSwain for his bride because she was the logical choice and for no other reason. Then, with the bitter taste of a lie in his mouth, he went to escort his date to their table for dinner.

"This should prove interesting," Christian said loud enough so only Ry could hear him. The trainer pulled out a chair for his date, a lovely brunette in a shimmering red gown, as his laughing eyes took in the group of people gathering at the large, round table.

Ry's brows slashed into a deep V over stormy eyes. Carter Hill had positioned himself directly across from Maggie. Short of making a scene that would undoubtedly get him thrown out of the Charlottesville hotel, there was nothing he could do about it. The banquet committee had made no formal seating arrangements. Also taking places at the table were Katie and Nick, who had come to see him accept an award from the VGA in honor of Rough Cut's brilliant career and pending retirement; Taylor Burwell, a wealthy retired businessman and investor in the Rough Cut syndicate; and Miss Emma Darlington.

Miss Emma wasted no time introducing herself to the distinguished Mr. Burwell, and seated herself beside him. Smiling, she leaned into him as she adjusted her napkin on the lap of her silver gray dress.

"Miss Emma," Ry said. "What a surprise to see you here."

"She told me she was coming to cruise for beefcake," Maggie whispered, earning a disgusted look from her date.

"The Darlingtons have always supported the equestrian sports," Miss Emma explained, cooling herself with an antique lace-and-ivory fan as she smiled coyly up at Burwell. "Our daddy, Jay Randolph Darlington, once jumped his horse through the crotch of a tree in Donner Park merely to gain the attention of a certain young lady. I was, myself, an avid equestrian for many years."

"Were you, my dear?" Burwell asked.

Miss Emma gave a throaty chuckle. "Why, you can't imagine the things I've done on horseback."

Ry choked a little on his drink and glared at Maggie, as if it was her fault for telling him Miss Emma had a rather randy nature.

The old woman's eyes took on a faraway gleam. "There was one time in particular—"

"It's a shame Mrs. Claiborne wasn't able to attend also," Maggie said, heading off what was undoubtedly another ribald tale.

Miss Emma shook her head. "She would have spent the entire evening worrying about Junior. She and that little dog have become inseparable. They'll both be at the show tomorrow. Will you be there, Mr. Burwell?"

Ry lost interest in the conversation when he caught Carter Hill gazing across the table at Maggie with calf eyes and his tongue all but hanging out of his mouth. He refrained from launching himself at the slender auburn-haired lawyer, managing to grind out a question instead. "On your own tonight, Hill?"

"Huh? Oh—a—yes. I'm afraid my date came down with something at the last minute."

"Terminal boredom, no doubt," Ry said under

his breath. He started to lean his elbows on the table, then pulled himself up short, looking like a moron. Carter Hill didn't put his elbows on the table.

Maggie sent a charming smile to her ex-beau. "I'm amazed you didn't have girls lined up to take her place, Carter."

Ry almost gagged.

"Well, I did have someone else in mind," Carter said, his gaze locked on her, "but she was already spoken for. Some other time perhaps."

Ry turned red and tensed in his chair, ready to pounce. Only Christian's hand on his arm kept him from bolting out of his seat.

The Englishman sent a smile across the table and smoothly changed the subject. "Can we expect to see you at the farm next month for the open house, Mr. Burwell?"

Maggie thought the dinner went rather well. Her nights of studying and Katie's tutoring paid off. She followed most of the conversation that went on around her. There was still plenty of hunter-jumper jargon to learn, but she didn't embarrass herself or Ry. She thought she succeeded in showing him she could fit into his world socially. That and driving him into a sexual frenzy had been her two goals for the evening. She was still working on the second one.

Most of the talk revolved around the topic of Ry's stallion. The horse was a product of the

Quaid Farm breeding program and was Ry's pride and joy. Maggie had learned that Rough Cut was the top money-winning horse in the history of grand prix jumping and would add another fifteen thousand dollars to his career earnings the next day if he jumped well in the Albemarle Cup Grand Prix.

"Do you think he'll do it, Christian?" Katie asked.

"If all goes according to plan."

Atherton's date gave him a saucy look. "Debutante and I may have something to say about that."

Christian's eyes glittered at the challenge. "Marissa is riding our top competition, Idlewylde Farm's Debutante," he explained. He winked at her. "Come now, love, you wouldn't spoil Rough Cut's grand finale, would you?"

Marissa smiled. "In a minute, and I wouldn't bat an eyelash. Rough Cut's worth a fortune whether he wins the Albemarle Cup or not."

"True," Ry said, salting his potatoes, "but fifteen grand would go a long way in paying for that new breeding shed we're putting up."

"I've heard the rumors on that syndication figure. My heart bleeds for you, Ry," Marissa said with no sympathy.

Christian shook his head as he sliced into his prime rib. "She's totally without mercy. I should know."

Everyone laughed at his comically pained expression.

"You should see all the improvements Ry is making at the farm in anticipation of Rough Cut's coming home to stand at stud, Mr. Burwell," Maggie said. She could feel Ry's gaze boring into the back of her head, and she smiled to herself. She winked at Katie, who had explained to her the expensive expansion of facilities that was going on at Quaid Farm. "In addition to the new breeding shed, there will be veterinary facilities on the grounds, and a new barn and paddocks for visiting mares. Isn't that right, sugar?" she asked, turning back to Ry.

"That's right," he said, thrown off balance by her wealth of knowledge. She had gone to some trouble to learn all that. Why?

Maggie patted his thigh under the table and every question he had flew right out of his head. The way she was sitting gave him an unobstructed view of her cleavage. He wondered vaguely if it wasn't against the law for a woman to wear a dress that numbed a man's brain so.

Maggie turned back to the conversation, leaving her hand on Ry's rock-hard thigh, her fingers absently massaging. Instead of making him relax, it had the exact opposite effect. The muscles tightened and tightened until she expected him to shoot out of the chair like a rocket.

"The expansion will be well worth the expense

if Rough Cut proves to be as good in the breeding pen as he is in the show ring," Burwell said.

"I'm sure you'll be glad you invested, Mr. Burwell. We're certain Rough Cut will live up to his potential as a sire," Maggie added.

Katie had also filled her in on what it meant to syndicate a stallion. She was extremely grateful, as the syndication of Rough Cut had been big news and hot gossip. Rumors ran the syndication price to seven figures.

Maggie thought she would bust from pride when the chairman of the Virginia Grand Prix Association called Ry to the front of the room to present him with a plaque and congratulate him for raising and campaigning a horse that had become a living legend in the sport. Ry had made it to the top of a very competitive business. She knew how hard he worked, how much he loved and sweated over his horses. To hear other people in the business sing his praises made her want to throw her arms around him and declare to everyone in the room that he was hers.

At the moment, she noted, he didn't look as though that would please him. He had returned to his seat and was wearing one of his infamous scowls as he watched Carter Hill reluctantly leave the table in search of a dancing partner.

"You weren't hiding behind any doors when they passed out charm, were you?" Ry's tone was anything but complimentary.

Maggie watched Christian and Marissa, and Katie and Nick step out onto the highly polished dance floor before she deigned to comment. She turned to Ry with a lazy smile as she chose a dark red grape from the plate of fruit at the center of the table. "I'm not quite sure how you mean that, sugar."

His scowl darkened from black to bottomless. "I mean, you've got all the men here panting after you like a pack of half-starved coon hounds. Carter Hill didn't take his eyes off you all through dinner."

"Didn't he?" she asked innocently, hiding her smile as she brought the grape to her lips and began slowly peeling it with her teeth. *Bless your jealous heart, Rylan Quaid.* "And why should you care, *friend?*"

Sweat filmed Ry's forehead. His train of thought momentarily derailed as he watched her small white teeth neatly strip the skin from the grape. "Hell . . . I-I don't. It's just that he's no man for you. You'd tear him to shreds inside of a week." The grape disappeared into her mouth. Her ripe red lips closed around it. He swallowed hard. "You need a man you can't intimidate."

"Is that a fact?" She glanced at him from the corner of her eyes as she lifted a fat, beautiful strawberry from the silver platter. Holding it between thumb and forefinger, she dunked the tip of it in her champagne glass, lifted it to her mouth, and licked the golden liquid off, her tongue lazily stroking the berry. Rylan went pale, then a blush began creeping up his thick neck from beneath the snow white collar of his shirt.

"Y-yeah, that's right," he mumbled, suddenly feeling as if there wasn't enough air in the room to fill a thimble, let alone his lungs. As she nipped the end off the strawberry, he felt every drop of blood in his body gravitate to one vital area. "You need a man with some backbone," he said hoarsely.

Maggie shifted on her chair. She'd never seduced a man. It was exciting. Watching him lose the struggle to maintain that damned steely control of his, knowing she was responsible, was turning her on. The tight bodice of her gown scraped against her hypersensitive nipples. Ry's hands would soothe that ache later.

Forcing her brain back to the conversation, she said, "A man like you?" She dipped the strawberry in the champagne once again and returned it to her lips. "I don't know about that, sugar. You were probably right; we're better off being friends. This way we can enjoy each other's company and still be—" she licked the strawberry again, "—open—" she took a bite, "—to other relationships."

The last of the berry disappeared, leaving only bright dots of red juice where she'd held it. Daintily she drew her tongue across the tip of her forefinger, then the pad of her thumb, her gaze locked on Ry's.

As she lowered her hand toward the platter again, aiming for a slice of peach, Ry's arm shot across the table with all the speed and power of a striking snake. His big hand manacled her wrist.

"Leave the fruit alone, Mary Margaret!"

Maggie drew her hand back, her eyes round with phony innocence. "Why Rylan, is something wrong?"

Nothing that couldn't be cured by pulling her naked onto his lap, he thought.

Damn. He had to cool out before they headed home, or his plan for the rest of the evening—not to mention the rest of his life—was going to be radically altered.

Without looking at Maggie, he excused himself and left the noise and heat of the ballroom behind. In the men's room, he bent over a marble sink and splashed cold water on his face, then stood staring into the mirror, water dripping off his nose and chin.

What the hell was the matter with him? He refused to let Christian's earlier statement answer that question. Lust was what was the matter with him. A few deep breaths, a little willpower, and he'd be fine. He drove a hand through his neatly combed hair, trying to compose himself. He'd be fine, he told himself, pulling his comb out of his pocket. He was feeling better already.

His new sense of calm vaporized the minute he returned to the ballroom. There was Maggie, on the dance floor with Carter Hill. A fine red mist clouded Ry's vision. Other relationships, she'd said! The hell if he was going to let a puny suit rack like Carter Hill get in the way of his marrying Maggie! The man didn't even own a decent horse!

He started toward them, visions of grievous bodily harm dancing in his head, until Miss Emma stepped in front of him.

"Why, Mr. Quaid, I've just been dying to dance with you all evening."

Ry ground his teeth as he lost sight of Maggie and Hill on the other side of the dance floor. He glanced down at the old woman as she took his hands and positioned them—one scandalously low on her hip. He pulled it up. "I'm not much for dancing, ma'am."

"Then it's high time you learned," she said, and started moving to the music.

He had no choice but to follow her and try to keep from mashing her dainty toes with his size thirteen feet.

"I'm so glad you're seeing more of our Mary Margaret. She's a lovely girl, so spirited. Much as I was at her age. Lord, the stories I could tell!" She gave him a naughty, knowing smile and let the subject drop as Maggie and Carter danced past. "I see you're letting her dance with that young Hill gentleman. How . . . *free-thinking* of you." She said it in that truly Southern way that used nothing more than slight emphasis to indicate disapproval. "I used to go out with his father. You wouldn't have thought there was much fire in him either, but I can tell you. . . .Well, it makes me blush to think of the things we used to do. He was particularly fond of a feather boa I used to own. . . ."

Maggie moved woodenly, standing as far away from Carter Hill as she could. She felt like a creep using Carter this way, and she blamed the feeling on Ry. Why did he have to be such a stubborn son of a gun? What was it about her that made him keep such a tight rein on his passions? She knew he found her desirable, so what was the problem and how could she cure it short of tying him up and attacking him? Hmm . . . tying him up. There was an idea that held immense potential for satisfaction. . . .

". . . but I'm going to be tied up," Carter's voice cut into her fantasy.

Maggie stared up at him, her dark eyes wide with surprise. "You do?"

"Do what?"

"Like to be tied up. Who would have guessed?"

He looked at her as if he thought she'd lost her mind entirely, too much the gentleman to ask her to explain. "I said, I was planning to attend the show tomorrow, but I'm going to be tied up. I'm working on a rather fascinating antitrust suit. . . ."

Her mind tuned out instantly. No, she wasn't going to feel bad about using Carter. She'd sat through too many dinners listening to his endless, boring explanations of his cases. He owed her.

Suddenly Ry's figure loomed up menacingly behind Hill. His big hand clamped down on the lawyer's shoulder, effectively halting their dance. He scowled into the man's aristocratically handsome face and said, "I'm cutting in."

Maggie was thrilled. Her temporary partner was not. Carter gave Ry a look of outrage, showing more gumption than anyone would have given him credit for. "Now see here, Quaid—"

Ry nearly lifted him off the floor with one hand. "Now you see here, Carter," he said in a dangerously silky voice, a malicious smile lifting his lips. "I won't have you pawing my date, dreaming up kinky things to do to her with a feather boa. You can let me cut in, or you can get your head soaked in the punch bowl."

Hill wisely took the first option. He backed off the dance floor, straightening his jacket and staring at Ry as if he were certain he had escaped a brush with a madman.

"I suppose that was rude," Ry said as he pulled a grinning Maggie into his arms.

She linked her hands behind his neck, loving the feel of his broad, hard shoulders. "Unpardonably. Why'd you do it?"

"You're *my* date." His voice dripped with possessive jealousy.

Maggie's stomach did a cartwheel. "But I didn't think you'd mind me dancing with another man since you and I are just friends."

"Well, I damn well mind if you dance with Carter Hill, and don't ask me why."

She decided to heed his warning, choosing instead to torment him by snuggling closer in his arms. "I swear, Rylan, sometimes I can't figure you out. What was that business about a feather boa?"

"Just something Miss Emma said. You wouldn't believe the story she told me." He blushed in remembrance.

"Was it kinky?"

His face darkened a shade.

Maggie chuckled. "Then I believe it."

He scowled at her as he shuffled his feet in the smallest concession to social dance. If she got any closer, they were going to create the biggest scandal in the history of the Virginia Grand Prix Association. He inched back away from her.

"You were certainly a fountain of information at dinner," he said dryly, latching on to a subject that couldn't possibly turn sexual in nature. "Why the sudden interest in my business?"

"I like to keep up on what my friends are doing. Do you have some objection to that?"

Objection? Did he have an objection to the

woman he wanted to marry taking an interest in the business that was his whole life? No. And it didn't matter if the only reason she was interested was the money, since he had been counting on the money from the syndication to help lure her into marriage with him in the first place. It was all part of the plan.

"No," he said, "no objections. I was just curious."

"So was I. Curious about you. I know how dedicated you are to the farm. I want to understand you better . . . friend." She said the word softly, earnestly, without the teasing quality in her voice she had been using all evening.

Ry's speculative gaze fell on an expression that was totally open, without guile. It was a look that caught at something in his chest, caught and hung on, even though a part of him wanted to back away from it.

Other couples moved around them, laughing and talking. Katie and Nick had found a corner near the bandstand to keep to themselves. Christian and Marissa danced by, their eyes locked in a combat Maggie would have found fascinating if she hadn't been so preoccupied with her own situation. Miss Emma and Taylor Burwell swept past doing the tango.

As the song ended, Maggie started to back out of Ry's embrace. "Thanks for the dance. I think I'll go powder my nose."

"No," he said, refusing to release her. He

lightened his tone at her startled look. "I don't want you more than an arm's length away from me while you're prancing around in that dress. Jeepers cripes, it's a wonder you didn't melt the ice sculpture when you walked past the head table."

"You like my dress, Ry?" she asked with a smile, stepping close again as the orchestra began another song.

He rolled his eyes.

Maggie drew one hand down the lapel of his jacket, smoothing her fingertips over the fine wool, feeling the solid strength of the muscle beneath. Lord help her, how she wanted this man! How she wanted him to hold her naked in his arms, loving her, letting her love him. In some primitive little corner of her mind she kept thinking if she could show him how much she loved him, if she could express that love physically, it would make it easier for him to fall in love with her.

Softly she asked, "Ry, are you as sick of being 'just friends' as I am?"

He didn't answer her. He didn't need to. Maggie could see his gaze heat, could feel that heat linger on her mouth, on the exposed upper slopes of her breasts. She wanted to melt against him, over him. *Cards-on-the-table time, Maggie.*

She leaned into him, raising on tiptoe to brush a kiss across his jaw, and whispered, "Let's go home, Ry. Take me home."

six

A STORM WAS gathering—outside the car and inside. As Ry piloted Maggie's Oldsmobile along the winding, climbing road toward Quaid Farm, lightning skittered across the night sky in spidery lines. Inside the car, brief looks and touches sizzled with promise. The electrical display heightened anticipation of the coming storms.

Maggie sat beside Ry reminding herself every few seconds that it wouldn't be a good idea to attack him while he was driving. She had waited a long time for this, she could wait a little longer. Still, it was impossible not to touch him. She had wanted to for so long, and he finally had given her permission by leading her out of the party at an indecently early hour. Neither of them had spoken a word since she'd asked him to take her home. They both knew where they were going and what was going to happen once they got there.

She leaned her head against his shoulder and bit her lip at the ache that was gnawing inside her. Her hand slid from her own thigh to his. His muscles were like iron, iron that began to quiver as her fingers moved upward.

Ry's hands tightened on the steering wheel until it was a wonder the thing didn't crack. He swore through his clenched teeth, his eyes riveted on the road ahead. "Jeepers cripes, Mary Margaret, if you move your hand another inch, I'm liable to drive us right off the damn road."

Her hand retreated, only to move up and slide inside his jacket. It took no imagination at all to picture him without the tux jacket and white shirt. She had seen him shirtless more than once as he worked around the farm, bulging, rippling muscles slick with sweat and gleaming under the sun. More than a hundred times she'd pictured him the same way arching over her as they made love. That dream was soon to become a reality.

What kind of lover would he be? She had dreamed dozens of different possibilities. Would he surprise her with his gentleness, or would his lovemaking be rough and earthy? What would he like? Where would he like to be touched? Would he be patient enough for teasing, or was his need as urgent as hers? She didn't have long to wait before finding out, she thought as they started down the driveway of Quaid Farm.

Ry tried to distract himself from the woman molding herself to his side. He tried to think of the thunderstorm that was brewing overhead, what the rain would do to the course at tomorrow's show. The wind had picked up considerably and was whipping at the bushes and trees, tumbling fallen leaves across their path. But the weather outside didn't seem nearly as turbulent as what was going on inside him, and his attention wandered back to Maggie.

Sweet Lord in heaven, how he wanted her! He wanted to stop the car and take her right there on the seat. He had walked her out of the party with her half in front of him so no one else could see how badly he wanted her. Now the wait was almost over, but if he didn't get a better handle on his control, it was going to be the first and last time he made love to Maggie. Seeing her in her new dress had not only aroused every molecule in his body, it had also reminded him of how soft and feminine she was. If he hurt her, he'd never forgive himself—and she'd never forgive him either.

What he needed was a few minutes to compose himself, a few minutes away from her, where he couldn't see her lush curves or feel her hands on his body or smell her perfume. Passion's Promise. Gosh almighty, why did he have to go remember that name now, he asked himself as parked the car and gritted his teeth against a surge of desire.

"Go on up to the house," he ordered Maggie without so much as glancing at her. "I have to check on something in the stables."

Hurt by his tone of voice, Maggie sat in the car and watched him stride across the yard and disappear into the first of the two dimly lit barns. How could he walk away like that? Who did he think he was, getting her all steamed up and then walking away? Something in the stables to check on? How about checking on her—she was about to experience spontaneous combustion from wanting him!

Tugging up the slipping bodice of her dress, Maggie slid out of the car and started across the yard, cursing her spike heels as she nearly turned an ankle walking across the gravel. The cold wind snatched at the skirt of her dress and wrapped its chilly fingers around her bare shoulders. Thunder rumbled overhead in warning. The storm was coming. Not even Rylan's dozen or so stray dogs were poking their noses out into the night.

Maggie stepped into the stable ready to light into Rylan, but the sound of his voice, low and soothing, stopped her. She stepped out of her shoes and quietly padded down the smooth, clean cement aisle with her heels dangling from the fingers of one hand.

Ry was in one of the box stalls. The door was open, and Maggie could see him squatting down in the stall, his head bent as he spoke. All the while, his hand moved in a slow, comforting rhythm along the neck of a foal that was curled up on the floor.

"You're gonna be all right, little guy. You're gonna be just fine. Your mama's gone, but we'll take care of you. Sure we will."

The tenderness in his voice hit Maggie broadside. Still unnoticed by Ry, she leaned against the door of the next stall, trembling with emotion. Here was the sweetness she had dreamed was inside him. It was real. It was there inside him hidden behind all the gruffness. Tears flooded her eyes, and a smile lifted her lips as she listened to him comfort the orphaned foal.

"What happened to his mama?" she asked softly, stepping into the doorway of the stall.

Ry glanced up at her and back to the foal. What must she think of him, leaving her in the car so he could come down to the barn and talk to his horses? No gentleman would have done that. Then again, no gentleman would have done what he would have done had he not left her in the car. Remarkably, she didn't look angry with him.

"Colic," he said, still feeling bad that he hadn't found the old mare in time to save her. "She died Wednesday. Left this little guy behind."

Maggie hitched her dress up with one hand and stepped into the stall. The colt was a bay with a star on his forehead and a snip on his nose and big, sad brown eyes. He lay in the fresh pine shavings that bedded the stall, his long, spindly legs tucked under him.

"We had a time getting him to suck from a bottle," Ry said, "but he's coming around. Your dress—" he started as Maggie awkwardly lowered herself to kneel by the baby's head.

"—will go to the cleaners Monday," she said, not giving a single thought to the fact that she had blown practically half her life's savings on the gown.

Here was a horse she wasn't afraid of. How could she be, he was just a baby. It was a perfect opportunity for her to get acquainted with the species. She let her hand follow Ry's down the colt's neck, over the slick, soft, blood red coat. "Why did you have to teach him to take a bottle? I thought it was about time to wean the foals anyway."

Ry's straight dark brows lifted in surprise. She'd been doing her homework. "It is. In fact, we weaned a bunch of the early babies a month ago already. But this little guy wasn't born until the end of June. Clever Trinket's last baby. She was Rough Cut's mama."

"Oh, Ry." Maggie laid a hand on his forearm, her brown eyes full of genuine sympathy. "I'm so sorry you lost her. She must have been very special to you."

He gave a little shrug, surprised at how deeply it touched him that she really cared. "She was a good old girl."

"Poor little sweetheart," Maggie crooned to the foal, scratching gently between his ears. The baby's eyes drifted shut at the same time Maggie began to shiver.

Ry slipped out of his jacket and draped it around her shoulders as he stood and drew her to her feet. "What you must think of me, keeping you out here in the cold. Let's go up to the house. I'll fix up something hot to drink."

"Will he be all right?" she questioned.

Ry smiled with a gentleness he wouldn't have credited himself with. "He'll be fine. Come on. Let's see if we can beat the rain to the front porch."

They couldn't.

They were halfway to the house when the sky opened up and drenched them. The rain poured down in sheets, soaking them instantly. Without breaking stride, Ry swung Maggie up in his arms and dashed for the front porch. When he set her down under the light in front of the door, they were both breathing hard and shaking the rain from their faces.

Maggie wanted to throw a tantrum. Her carefully arranged hairstyle was now plastered to her head. The makeup she had brushed on with an artist's care had been washed off in the downpour. The image she had worked on so hard to seduce Rylan with was gone. She looked up at him expecting the flame of desire in his eyes to have been thoroughly doused.

What she saw in his eyes was need and passion. The harsh lines of his face seemed cut from stone as he stared down at her, the flame of desire burning even brighter than it had at the party.

He was soaked as well. His dark hair was slicked to his head, accenting the high, hard cheekbones, the narrow, watchful eyes, the bold nose, the wide, sensuous mouth. He looked fierce and hungry, and a bolt of anticipation shot through Maggie with more force than if it had been lightning.

The white tuxedo shirt clung to Ry's broad shoulders, transparent in its wetness. He had shed his bow tie the instant they'd left the party and popped open the first two buttons on his shirt. Now raindrops clung to and nestled in the dark curls of his chest hair.

Slowly, as if mesmerized, Maggie reached a hand up and touched one crystalline drop with the tip of her finger. The tuxedo jacket slipped back on her bare shoulders, then dropped off. Ry caught hold of her, his big hand circling her wrist, drawing her arm down to the side. Then his hands were on her cheeks, holding her face as he bent his head and kissed her.

The kiss was wild. There was no token show of control from either of them. As the storm broke around them they stood under the shelter of the porch, out of the rain and wind, but battered by their own storm, the storm of desire that had been building for weeks. As thunder crashed over-head, Ry's mouth slanted across Maggie's, hot and wet. His tongue slid against hers, branding her, staking his claim, teasing her with the kind of strokes that imitated more intimate contact.

She met fire with fire, kissing him back with

equal fervor. Her tongue dueled with his as her hands dragged his shirttail from his pants then slid beneath to caress the slick, steely muscles of his back. Her teeth grazed his lower lip. He groaned deep in his throat and kissed her harder, bruising her lips as he bent her back over his arm. His other hand came between them to stroke the exposed skin above her gown. Then his fingers curled inside the bodice, and he tugged it down.

Maggie moaned as her breasts sprang free, one into Ry's waiting hand. He kneaded the full round globe aggressively, almost roughly. His thumb found her already distended nipple and stroked it until the pleasure became so intense, it bordered on pain.

Needing to touch him, Maggie's trembling fingers caught in the opening of his shirt. Buttons flew and bounced on the floor like tiny hailstones as she tore the garment open. Greedily her hands roamed the vast planes of his chest, delighting in the warmth of his skin, the crisp texture of the hair that covered it, the flex and strain of his muscles.

"Ah, Maggie," he said with a groan, his voice as rough as gravel as he dragged his lips along her jaw to her ear. "I want you so bad. I want to taste you. I want your breast in my mouth."

"Oh, Ry, yes." She whimpered. Desire hummed through her body until every nerve ending vibrated with it. "I want that too."

What little control he had left was vaporized by

the raw desire in her voice. He kissed her again as he straightened and took a step backward. His legs hit the seat of the old bentwood rocker that had been on the porch as long as he could remember. He sat down on it, pulling Maggie with him so that she half sprawled across him, one foot remaining on the floor, one knee skidding across his thigh. Her hands went out automatically to save herself and landed against the wall on either side of his head, her breast thrust directly into his mouth.

He welcomed the eager peak, loving it with his lips, tongue, teeth. He kissed the very tip, then drew it into his mouth, sucking hard, wringing a cry of pleasure from her. His hands, meanwhile, had found their way into the slit of her gown, and his big fingers fumbled with the tabs of her garters. Their hands collided on her left thigh as Maggie reached down to help him. She stroked his forearm with her fingertips then curled her fingers around his wrist and held his hand against her satiny inner thigh when he started to draw it back.

"Touch me," she whispered, unable to take in enough air to do more than that. "Touch me, Ry, please."

As his mouth sought out her other breast she guided his hand up her thigh, then sighed and moaned as he cupped her through her lace panties.

It was too much, Ry thought, to touch her this way, to see, feel, and hear her respond, and not have all of her. His fingers slipped inside the leg of her panties, seeking out the soft heat of her womanhood. He found her ready for him, eager for him, practically begging for him as her hips began to move.

The decision was made. Not consciously, because he was well beyond conscious thought, but on a basic level where there was only male and female and a need that raged out of control.

Muttering a stream of hot, blue words, Ry worked down the fly of his trousers.

"Oh, Ry." Her lips moved against his wet dark hair as she arched against him. "Now. Please, now."

Too urgent to wait any longer, he tugged her panties aside and pulled her onto his lap, his big hands bracketing her hips and working up the skirt of her dress. He entered her forcefully, his need to be enclosed by her tight hot warmth shutting out all else, including her sharp cry.

Maggie's fingers bit into the muscles of Ry's shoulders as she was impaled on him. The sensation was powerful, painful, wonderful. Her body was full of him, achingly full, magnificently full. She finally knew what it was to be possessed by this man she had loved for so long. It was nothing less than she had dreamed, nothing less than perfect. These thoughts passed through her mind very clearly but very quickly as need took over.

She began to move on him. He arched up to meet her. The old bentwood chair rocked beneath them, adding a unique extra sensation to the proceedings.

Their loving was hard and fast, almost desperate in its intensity. At first Ry held Maggie as she rode him, then, still buried deep inside her, he lowered them both to the floor of the porch. Maggie gasped at the feel of cool smooth wood against her back. She gasped at the feel of Ry driving into her, seeking the same blinding flash of pleasure she felt rushing toward her. When it came, it took her breath away and filled her head with a brilliant white light that made the lightning around them seem dim by comparison.

Ry felt her go rigid beneath him, felt the waves of completion tighten her body around his. That was all it took to send him shooting over the edge.

It might have been five minutes or it might have been an hour before he got his breath back, before reality burned off the haze of sexual desire that had totally fogged his brain. Resting on his elbows, he looked down at Maggie. She was breathing hard, her head turned toward the yard where the rain had let up already and now fell in a soft, steady shower. Her eyes were nearly closed, her love-bruised lips were parted slightly, her cheeks glistened with tears.

Tears.

"Oh, Lord," he whispered under his breath. "What have I done?"

He reached up to brush the moisture from her cheek with the back of his hand. Maggie sighed but didn't turn to look at him. Easing out of her and off of her, Ry rose to his feet, zipping his pants. He turned away from her, running his hands back over his wet hair. "Sweet heaven, what have I done?"

Maggie stared up at him, bewildered. What had he done? He'd just made her the happiest, most sexually satisfied woman on earth—possibly in the universe. She wanted to say so, but she wasn't capable of stringing that many words together yet.

Ry, on the other hand, while he might have been satisfied, did not look happy. In fact, he looked distinctly *un*happy. Maggie never took her eyes off him as she sat up and tugged the bodice of her gown back into place. He stood staring out at the rain-spattered night, head bent, hands clamped at his waist, one leg cocked slightly to the side. His expression was that of a man who had just made the worst mistake of his life.

A cold knot of fear clenched in Maggie's stomach like a fist. She pushed herself to her feet, grabbing up Rylan's dinner jacket to huddle into against the chill she hadn't noticed when they'd been making love. She wanted to go to him, to touch him, but uncertainty held her back. Instead she managed to put all the questions in her heart into one word.

"Ry?"

He flinched. Lord, he could hear the tears in her voice. She sounded weak and frightened and hurt. This was his worst nightmare come true. This was the very thing he'd been fighting his libido to avoid. He damned himself to hell and gone. How could he have been such a bastard? Now he would lose her, almost certainly. Hell, he deserved to lose her.

Maggie took a hesitant step closer. "Rylan?"

"Maggie, I'm sorry," he said in a tortured whisper. "I'm so sorry."

"Sorry?" She tried to swallow down the panic fluttering in her throat. She pulled his coat tighter around her, shoving the sleeves up to expose her hands.

For a moment he said nothing. He stood there listening to the rain on the tin roof and calling himself a fool. "I should never have let that happen."

"Don't say that!" Maggie grabbed his arm and yanked on it, meaning to turn him to face her. Of course she couldn't budge him, but she surprised him into doing her bidding. He looked down at a face blazing with feminine fury. She imagined she looked slightly ridiculous swallowed up in his jacket. A lock of fire red hair fell across her forehead. She raked it back angrily and smacked a fist against Ry's bare chest. "Damn you, Rylan

Quaid, don't you dare say we shouldn't have made love!"

Confusion clouded his stormy eyes.

She shoved up the coat sleeve and smacked him again. "Don't you dare tell me you didn't want me!"

Ry caught her fist before she could hit him again. "Didn't want you? Maggie, what the blue blazes are you talking about? I wanted you so bad, I took you without a thought in my head. I wouldn't blame you a bit if you never wanted to see me again after that performance. Cripes almighty, I acted like I hadn't been near a woman in years! That wasn't at all how I meant for the evening to end."

It was Maggie's turn to be confused. Her hands dropped to her sides and immediately disappeared inside the coat sleeves. "You *did* want me?"

Hitching his hands to his hips, Ry snorted. "I thought I made that more than obvious."

Maggie shook her head as if the action might make all the pieces of the bizarre puzzle fall into place. "You wanted me. I wanted you. What are we arguing about?"

"Maggie, I hurt you! And, heaven above, I didn't even have the decency to wait until I got you in the house!" He took her face in his hands and stared down at her with such remorse in his eyes, it made Maggie's heart ache. "I hurt you. Lord, baby, I am so *so* sorry."

His apology touched her in a way nothing else ever had. This big tough man who seldom showed any emotion other than orneriness was afraid he might have hurt her.

"Oh, Ry," she whispered, slipping her arms around his waist and pressing her cheek to the sweat-dampened curls on his chest. "I'm all right. I'm better than all right."

Ry wrapped an arm around her and stroked his other hand over her hair, holding her now as tenderly as he wished he had earlier. "But I was so rough with you. I know I hurt you, Maggie. I saw the tears on your face."

"Sugar, ladies cry when they're happy too." She smiled up at him. "Don't you know how much you pleased me, how much I needed you?"

He scowled, seeming determined to rake himself over the coals some more. "I took you on the front porch. On the damn front porch, for cripes sakes!"

"Did you hear me complaining? I distinctly remember uttering nothing more than sighs and moans of ecstasy."

"I lost control."

"Finally." She rolled her eyes and heaved a sigh of supreme relief. "Praise the Lord."

"Carter Hill wouldn't have made love to you on the front porch."

"Sugar, I have serious doubts Carter Hill could find his way out of his shorts without a map. You didn't have any trouble with that—for which I am *extremely* grateful." Loving him more than ever, Maggie lifted her hand to his cheek where his beard was beginning to shadow his cleanly shaven skin. "Oh, Rylan, don't you know what it does to me to know you wanted me so badly you lost control?"

His broad shoulders lifted in a self-conscious shrug. "No," he mumbled. He had been so sure she would think he was a lout, an uncouth, uncivilized lout.

Maggie arched against him like a cat, running her flattened palm over his chest. She gave him the most sultry, seductive look in her repertoire. "It makes me *so* hot, Rylan."

"Jeepers cripes, Mary Margaret, you say the damnedest things." An embarrassed little grin tugged at the corners of his mouth as he blushed under the soft glow of the porch light.

Maggie chuckled and shook her head. He was so cute. This was the same man who had growled some very naughty words in her ear as he'd made love to her. Now he was blushing because she was admitting how excited that made her.

"Well, it does," she said. She let her hand trail down his side and started bringing it back up again, dragging her fingers along his leg.

Ry sucked in his breath. Damn, but she turned him on. And she enjoyed doing it, too, the little minx. He gave her a roguish smile, totally abandoning the sudden shyness that had brought ruddy color to his cheeks only a moment ago. "Do tell. Why don't we go inside and discuss this further?"

Maggie's eyes were smoldering as her gaze locked with his. "Will you show me how you meant for the evening to end?"

"As many times as you want."

Maggie had never felt more cherished in her life. Ry had indeed planned an ending for their evening—a very romantic ending. He had turned down the covers of his bed and placed a rose on one pillow. He had a bottle of wine and two glasses sitting on one nightstand and a trio of candles in brass candlesticks on the other. All this, not because he was a romantic sort of man—he wasn't—but because he had thought she would want it.

Seeing all the preparations, she smiled—not just with her lips but with her heart as well. If Ry had taken the time and trouble to do all this, surely it meant he cared deeply for her. If he wanted her as badly as he had on the porch and cared enough to put a rose on her pillow, surely it was possible he was beginning to love her. She thought of how jealous he'd been when the other men at the party had paid attention to her, and her smile deepened another notch.

"You did all this for me," she stated, turning to face him at the end of the bed. While she'd been in the bathroom trying to restore some order to her hair, Ry had lit the candles. They combined their light with that of a small brass lamp in the far corner to bathe the room in a soft glow.

Ry slipped his jacket from her shoulders and tossed it to a nearby chair. "I wanted it to be special for you, Maggie."

He was willing to admit that much. He wasn't willing to admit even to himself that *he* wanted to be special to her as well. In fact, he would have flat-out denied it. His rationalization was that in order to get Maggie to agree to be his wife, he would have to treat her the way she expected to be treated, the way an admiral's daughter expected to be treated.

"Making love with you would be special any way," Maggie said, a little nervous at having divulged that much of herself. It was one thing to love Ry and keep that secret locked in her heart. It was quite another to admit it to him when she was still uncertain of where she stood with him.

She reached up to tug his damp shirt back off his shoulders. It joined the jacket on the chair. Giving in to compulsive need, she ran her hands down his chest, then wrapped her arms around him and hugged him. "I've wanted you so badly for so long."

He didn't ask how long. She would have to have said forever. For as long as she'd been a grown woman, he'd been the man of her dreams.

Ry was becoming too caught up in desire to question anything she said. She was so soft in his arms. Her scent drifted up to tease his nostrils: perfume and woman, rain and lovemaking. There was a sense of rightness at having her in his house, in his bedroom, that went way beyond his convenient excuse of practicality, but he ignored it in his typically hardheaded fashion. He concentrated on Maggie instead.

After a rather pleasant search, his fingers found the zipper hidden in the side of her dress. He lowered it, then peeled the dress off her, uncovering her inch by inch, kissing his way down her body until he was on his knees and the gown was a puddle of teal silk and sequins on the blue rug. Maggie's hands tangled in his hair as he rid her of her garter belt and stockings, then eased her lace panties down her hips, once again letting his lips trail behind his fingers. She leaned into him, her breath catching as his tongue explored the delicate territory between her legs. Then she was in his arms again.

He kissed her hair as his hands roamed over her back and down to her hips. He lifted her and fitted her against the hardness that strained the fly of his trousers and whispered hotly in her ear. "You taste so good, Maggie. So sweet." Then his lips found hers and shared that taste with her.

Their loving this time was slow and sweet. The urgency had burned off leaving behind a glowing core of desire, a fire that burned long into the night.

Ry worshiped Maggie's body, kissing, caressing, praising with words and without. She was so womanly, it made him ache just looking at her. Her breasts filled his hands, dusky peach nipples pouted for attention from his mouth. His teeth nibbled at her nipped-in waist. His fingers traced the graceful swell of her hips, slipped beneath to squeeze her well-rounded derriere.

Maggie took equal delight in discovering the secrets of Ry's big body. He had the kind of physique other men joined athletic clubs in search of. All six feet four inches of him was thick, solid muscle, liberally dusted with rough dark hair. She found he liked to have her hands and mouth on his upper body, while other parts of him were less tolerant of teasing.

"Mag-gie," he said in a warning tone as her fingertips grazed his inner thigh.

"Don't you like that, Rylan? Maybe you'll like this better."

He growled, grabbed her hands, and pinned them above her head pressing her down into the mattress with his body. Nose to nose, their gazes locked, full of dares and promises to make good on them.

"Do you know what I'm going to do to you if you don't stop teasing me?"

"What?" she questioned breathlessly. She

wouldn't have thought it possible, but she felt her entire body grow hotter as Ry dipped his head and whispered his intentions in her ear, not sparing any erotic detail. Tiny shivers of anticipation graduated to full-fledged trembling. "Mmm . . ." She moaned. "Is that a threat . . . or a promise?"

Still holding her hands and her gaze, Ry slid into her welcoming warmth, reaching deep enough to make her gasp.

"Let me touch you," Maggie begged, trying to free her arms as Ry eased out of her.

"No." His next thrust was a little stronger. Maggie's body arched to meet him.

"Ry, let me go."

"No." He repeated the process again.

"You devil."

He chuckled.

She groaned.

"Rylan . . ."

"No."

"Oh—ooh—Rylan . . . yes, yes, yes."

"Ah—yes—oh, Maggie."

The candles had gone out. It didn't matter. The approaching dawn was turning the sky outside his bedroom window pale pearl gray. Enough soft, misty light spilled in for Ry to study the woman lying in his arms.

Damn, it felt good to have her there. She cuddled against him, one arm banded across his chest, her legs tangled with his, her soft round cheek pressed to the hollow of his shoulder. He stroked a hand over her tangle of dark copper hair. It wasn't going to be any hardship getting used to holding her this way.

A strange warmth wandered around inside his chest at the thought of waking up every day with Maggie snuggling up to him. To avoid thinking about it, he turned his attention to a new topic.

How long should he wait before he proposed to her again? It seemed their compatibility should be fairly obvious to Maggie after the night they'd just spent. Holy cow, he'd never known it was possible for two people to be *that* compatible. Aside from their delightful discovery, she was beginning to show an interest in the farm. The party they had attended had given her a glimpse of the glamorous side of the show-jumping world. The gossip floating around the ballroom had certainly given her an idea of the financial position he would be in once the syndication of Rough Cut was complete. She should be convinced by now that marrying him would be mutually beneficial.

Maybe he would propose to her today. He imagined the perfect scenario: Rough Cut would win the Albemarle Cup; Ry would invite Maggie to join him at the awards presentation, and after he'd accepted the trophy and prize money check, he would propose to her. The scene brought a smile to his lips. He'd have his prize stallion on one side and his bride-to-be on the other. Life didn't get much better than that.

Maggie stirred in her sleep, rubbing her head against him like a kitten. As he tugged the covers up around her shoulders, an incredible wave of tenderness swept over him. Had he been standing, Ry was certain it would have knocked him flat on his back. The element of surprise was outweighed only by the rising sense of panic that seemed to grab him by the throat. He fought it off. Why should he feel panicky? Everything was going exactly according to his plan.

Then Maggie stretched and raised her head. She pushed her hair out of her eyes and gave him a smile that would have warmed the coldest heart. Her sable eyes sparkled at him with remembrance of the night before and glowed with something he didn't attempt to identify. She reached up to touch his whisker-rough cheek and turned his whole world upside down with three little words.

"I love you."

seven

MAGGIE COULDN'T HAVE said exactly what she had expected Ry's reaction to be. He might have given her a warm smile. He might have blushed and scowled at her, then dragged her up and kissed her. Both fantasies had floated through her dreams. Both had ended with him making love to her. Neither had included the look he was giving her now—surprised, guarded, regretful.

It was the regret that hurt most, Maggie decided, pushing herself up in bed, holding the sheet up to cover herself as she did so. Surprise was a natural reaction to hearing those words from someone for the first time. And she had expected a certain amount of caution from him. His past relationships had made him wary. But regret . . . oh, man, that hurt, because there was no comforting explanation for it. Regret was regret, and though her mind scrambled frantically, nothing she could think of could soften the blow.

Ry didn't want her love.

"Well," she said, a knot of tears lodged in the middle of her throat like a walnut in the shell. She fussed with the bed covers, gathering the material by the fistful and pulling it up around her. Her gaze dodged away from Ry's. "It seems I said the wrong thing, didn't I?"

Ry pushed himself up and leaned back against the headboard, the sheet pooling below his waist. He looked tough and tousled with his dark hair mussed around his head and the shadow of his beard graying the hard angular planes of his cheeks. "Maggie, don't confuse great sex with love."

Anger washed her face a vibrant shade of red.

She glared at him, open-mouthed. After all these years, she'd finally told him she loved him, and he had to come up with a line like that! "I'm not confused," she said, her voice shaking with rage, "but apparently you are."

She stepped off the bed, dragging the covers with her as she went in search of her clothes, leaving Rylan on the bed, buck naked.

"Maggie, what are you doing?" he demanded, climbing out of bed to follow her around the room. In a concession to modesty, he snatched his white cotton briefs off the back of a chair and held them in front of himself.

"I'm *hic* going home." She picked up her garter belt and a lone stocking, wadded them into a ball, and stuffed them into one of her shoes. Glancing back at Rylan, she frowned at his attempt to cover himself. "Sugar, isn't that a little *hic* like trying to hide a baseball bat with a postage stamp?"

Ry scowled. He stepped into his shorts as Maggie returned to her search. "Maggie, I didn't mean to hurt your feelings."

"Didn't you?" She gave a half laugh as she reached partway under the bed for her panties. "Well, that's a shame, darlin', because you scored a bull's-eye."

Knowledge that he'd hurt her was like a knife in Ry's chest. He had only wanted to set her straight to help her avoid getting hurt in the future. They had spent a fantastic night together; she was in love with the way he'd made her feel. She wasn't in love with him.

As if in answer to his thoughts, she wheeled on him, shaking a shoe in his face. "I'm a grown *hic* woman, Rylan Quaid. I know the difference between love and multiple orgasms. I know I'm in *hic* love with you. If you can't handle that, it's just too damn bad, but don't you dare throw it back in my face!"

She started for the door, intending to go down the hall to the bathroom to dress, but Ry stepped on the bedclothes trailing behind her, then caught her by the shoulders and pulled her back against him.

"All right, all right," he said impatiently. "I'm sorry."

If she wanted to think she was in love with him, who was he to stop her? As she'd said, she was a grown woman, responsible for her own actions, for her own feelings. His responsibility was to himself, to keep his own head clear, to keep things in their proper perspective. He knew better than to believe in the love she thought she felt; it was just a passing thing.

Maggie struggled against his hold a bit, fighting his superior strength in vain. Ry wrapped his arms around her, pulling her back against his chest. There were times when he enjoyed having her hiss and spit at him like an angry cat. But now he felt a strong need to hold her and soothe the hurt he'd caused. It was a need he didn't examine too closely.

"Sometimes you make me so doggone mad, Rylan." Her temper had kept her tears at bay. His sudden tenderness was loosening her tight hold on control, making her mouth tremble and eyes fill up and overflow.

"I know. I'm a bastard," he said softly. He pressed a whisper-soft kiss in her tangled hair then nuzzled through the dark burnished mass to brush another on her neck. "I'm just a big, rough farmer. Wouldn't know charm if it spit in my face."

Maggie sniffled and scrubbed at a tear with the heel of her hand, a watery chuckle escaping her. "That's a fact." Twisting around, she pressed her cheek to his chest as the tears began coming in earnest. Hugging him for all she was worth, she said, "But I love you anyway."

"Shhh . . . shhh . . ." Ry held her tight, rocking her back and forth, drinking in the feel of her sweet soft curves in his arms. A hint of her perfume still teased his nostrils. She was very feminine, and she seemed as fragile as a flower crying in his arms. Like a knife through silk, the sound tore through him all the way to his soul. He held her tighter. "Hush, baby, please don't cry."

"I-I-I love you, and y-you don't believe me."

That wasn't the stuff her dreams had been made of. In her dreams Ry had always returned her declaration of love with one of his own. His silence now squeezed around her heart like a fist, but she took hope in the comfort he offered. When his palms pressed against her cheeks, she raised her head and accepted the kisses he feathered across her face to take her tears away. When he pressed his lips to hers, she accepted that kiss too.

She loved him. It seemed she'd always loved him. So what choice did she have but to try to make him believe in that love? She put everything she was feeling into her kiss, refusing to stop even when he lifted her in his arms and the bedclothes she had wrapped around her fell away. She offered herself to him freely, without reservation, with all the love that ached in her heart. She stroked her love along the sleek, hard lines of his back, wrapped it around his hips, gloved the essence of his maleness with it. And when they reached passion's summit, she whispered it to him from the very depths of her being.

"Marry me, Maggie."

Her lips lifted in a tired smile as she zipped her dress. "I guess that's an improvement over your last proposal."

"Good enough for an admiral's daughter?" Dressed in jeans and a white western shirt, Ry stood by his dresser fiddling with the articles that sat on top, watching Maggie in the mirror. He didn't pursue the topic when she chose to ignore the question. It hardly seemed relevant anymore.

If she thought she was in love with him, she probably thought he was good enough for her. In any case, the promise of the money and notoriety Rough Cut was bringing home was enough to make up for his own rough edges. "We make a good team."

"Like Siskel and Ebert? Abbott and Costello? Pork rinds and beer?" she joked, trying to keep an eye on him as she bent to force her foot into her shoe.

Ry didn't laugh. "I mean it. I'm sick of playing these little games."

"Okay." She straightened and smoothed her skirt, nerves dancing in her stomach. "No more games then. Do you love me, Ry?"

He stiffened, avoiding his own reflection in the mirror. Did he love her? No. He was attracted to her, liked her, and respected her. . . . Christian Atherton's words of the night before came hauntingly to mind: *All those things add up to love.*

Only if you're fool enough to let them, a bitter little voice murmured inside him. He'd seen his father do it, he'd nearly done it himself once, and once was enough. He wanted Maggie, but he was going to be honest about it with her. He wouldn't be a fool for love again. He couldn't be. He just didn't have it in him.

He turned to face her and heaved a sigh, his big shoulders sagging. "It's just a word, Maggie."

"Not in my book it isn't."

"We've got so much going for us. Don't screw it up waiting for some abstract concept to make bells ring in your head." Determined to sway her to his way of thinking, he started ticking off his points on his fingers. "We're attracted to each other. We like each other—most of the time—"

She sliced her hand through the air to cut him off. "If you're going to read me that damn list again, I swear I'll choke you. We're people, Rylan, human beings, not critters with pedigrees to be matched up and bred in hopes of a nice foal crop."

"I do not think of you as a brood mare," he said, dropping his hands to his slim hips. "I think we could have a good life together, and I'm sick of waiting to get started on it. Marry me."

She could have pointed out that he was being arrogant and dictatorial, but that would have been a waste of breath. He had no doubt been born arrogant and dictatorial. He had probably bossed around the nurses in the delivery room at his birth. And the truth of the matter was, she liked him that way. Once they were married, it was going to be one contest of wills after another, which suited her fine. There was just one little thing she wanted, one thing she had to have cleared up first.

She stepped closer to him, looked up into the fierce expression she loved so much, and wished that for once things would go according to her dreams. "Do you love me?"

"Aw, Maggie." All the fight drained out of him on his sigh. The regret was there in his eyes again as he lifted a hand and stroked her cheek. "Don't ask me for something I'm not capable of. If there ever was a part of me that could feel that way, it died a long time ago. I'll give you everything else you ever wanted, honey."

"But not your love."

"You can't go to the well if the darn thing is dry."

If she had believed that were true, that he simply wasn't capable of giving love, Maggie could have walked away from him feeling nothing more than pity. But it wasn't true, and she knew it. Ry had love in him. She'd seen him give it to his sister, to his horses, to the strays he took in. He gave it to her in his own stubborn way. He undoubtedly called it something else, but it was love.

She had lain awake half the night thinking it over, and she was convinced Ry was in love with her. He exhibited every known symptom. He admitted to each individual one. And no man would display as much jealousy as he did if there weren't deeper feelings involved. As far as she was concerned, the question now wasn't whether or not he was capable of loving, but whether or not he could let go of his fears and admit his love to her and to himself.

"Maggie, you know I care about you, you know I want you. We could have a good life together. Can't we leave it at that?"

Leave it at that? When she had loved him forever and had dreamed of nothing but his loving her in return? No, she couldn't leave it at that. She wouldn't settle for that when she knew in her heart of hearts they could have it all. They deserved better than to leave it at wanting and caring. And, because she loved him so, she felt she owed it to him to show him he could love and be loved and not get his heart broken in the process.

"Oh, Rylan," she said on a sigh. Shaking her head wearily, she slid her arms around him and hugged him. "What am I going to do with you?"

"Marry me." He scowled at her as if he thought he could get her to say yes by sheer force of will.

She raised up on tiptoe to kiss his nose. Her smile was as soft as satin. "I love you." She stepped back and ran a hand over her skirt. "I'd better get on home so I can change clothes. Silk and sequins are probably overdressing for a horse show."

When she was halfway to the door, he said, "You didn't answer me, Mary Margaret."

The look she gave him was tender but run through with threads of firm resolve. "You'll get the answer you want, Ry, when I get the one I need to hear."

Without another word she went downstairs and out the front door onto the wide porch, stopping at the view that greeted her. The sun had just cleared the eastern horizon, and the mists had yet to burn off the lower-lying land. A sense of peace and stillness embraced the farm. The weekend help had yet to arrive to start morning chores, so the only sounds drifting up from the stables were occasional low whinnies.

Tears stung her eyes. Oh, how she loved him, and how badly he needed that love.

This farm was where she wanted to spend the rest of her life. This was where she wanted to raise her children—Ry's children. She could easily picture herself coming out onto this porch in the morning with a cup of coffee, absorbing the solitude as she sat and rocked in the old bentwood rocker—the rocker they had made love on, she recalled with heat in her cheeks. She could see their children playing on the lawn—a pair of sturdy little boys and their red-haired baby sister. She could imagine standing there in the evening, watching Ry walk up from the stables in his dusty jeans and battered boots.

They could have that together—a home, a family, the kind of security based on a solid foundation of love. They would have it. She would see to it.

Shivering in the chilly fall air, Maggie crossed the yard to the main barn. She ignored the dogs that came looking for attention and pulled one of Ry's work jackets off a peg on the wall. It swallowed her up, the sleeves falling beyond her fingertips and the hem nearly to her knees. She welcomed the warmth of the soft flannel lining as well as the scent of horses and hay and Rylan. She didn't even mind the faintly lingering aroma of that awful liniment.

For someone who had just been told she could never have the only thing she'd ever wanted—Ry's love—she was in an amazingly good mood, Maggie mused. Perhaps that was because, in spite of everything, she was more convinced than ever that she would indeed have what she had dreamed of. It was going to take some work, and it wasn't going to be easy, but then nothing worth having ever was. Besides, she had never been one to shrink from a challenge. She wasn't an admiral's daughter for nothing.

Hugging herself, she walked down the wide aisle, smiling as the horses greeted her with hungry nickers. She stopped at the stall of the orphaned foal and slid the door back. The baby hopped up on his stiltlike legs and pranced toward her, his velvety muzzle reaching out, worried brown eyes alight with curiosity. Maggie smiled. His larger relatives might make her want to turn tail and run, but she couldn't muster even a tiny sliver of fear faced with this little guy.

"Hi, sweetie," she cooed, reaching out to let him sniff at her hand. "You little darlin'. You and I are going to be good friends."

The colt stepped closer, peeking out the opened door and calling for his absent mother with a shrill, frightened whinny.

"Poor baby," Maggie said, scratching his neck. "You need love about as much as your big ornery master does, don't you?"

On her way out of the barn Maggie snuck a peek in the dispensary, chuckling to herself at the sight of a big golden retriever sprawled on a red plaid cushion with a dozen snub-nosed pups nursing at her side. The dog had been groomed and a shiny new tag hung from her collar. Maggie thought of the man who had taken the animal in, cared for her, and would be tripping over the passel of puppies that no one else had wanted.

"And he thinks he's not capable of loving." Maggie shook her head. "Rylan Quaid, you have got another think coming."

Rough Cut was a lot like his master: big, athletic, and arrogant. He was enormous, a word that translated to seventeen hands in horse jargon. Muscles rippled beneath his shining copper coat with his slightest movement. He stood, quiet but alert, gazing off into the distance as a groom efficiently braided his black mane. He looked like a handsome young prince, bored with and detached from the attentions of his personal servants.

He was unquestionably a beautiful creature, Maggie thought. She stood a safe distance outside the stall, watching the two grooms prepare him for the show ring. While one worked at the intricate task of braiding, the other began the process of tacking up, settling the pad and saddle on the big horse's back.

The barn was alive with activity, the air filled with noise and excitement. A boom box pumped out Elton John's latest hit as an announcement for the next class was called out on the PA system. Voices ranged from joking to curt to angry. They mingled with whinnies and the clomping of steel-shod hooves on the concrete as horses were led in from and out to the show grounds.

Maggie remembered many of the sights and sounds from the days when Katie had competed. Indeed, she had first spotted Ry's line of stalls by the royal blue drapes and chrome-trimmed tack trunks of Quaid Farm. As had been the case back then, everything was in its place. The floor had recently been swept. The outer wall of one stall was decorated with ribbons that had been won by Quaid Farm horses during the first two days of the show. A smile of pride touched Maggie's mouth; after all, they were going to be her horses too.

"Well, hell, Mary Margaret," Ry said, rounding the corner of the stalls. With no more greeting than that he grabbed her hand and pulled her toward the stall where Rough Cut was being prepared. "Don't be shy. Come meet the meal ticket."

She swallowed the protest in her throat. She was going to conquer her fear. She was going to show Ry she was more than willing to fit into his life. Still, she stayed a little bit behind him as they stepped into the stall and approached the horse.

"He's a gentleman, but mind where you put your fingers, cause he'll nip if he thinks he can get away with it."

Maggie glanced at the horse's mouth, then at her fingers. They were short enough as it was. She jumped when the horse gave a sudden low nicker, and was glad Ry was too busy digging in his pocket to notice her show of nerves.

"Hey, Cutter, old pal," Ry said, fishing out a butter mint and offering it to the horse on his open palm. "You gonna pay off the loan on that new breeding shed today?"

"Don't fill his head with business pressures, old man," Christian said, coming out of the tack stall adjusting his necktie at the throat of his white shirt. He was already in white breeches and tall black boots, needing only his jacket and hard hat to complete his outfit. He winked at Maggie and said, "Remind him of all the lovely ladies that are going to come calling next spring."

Marissa McLaughlin sauntered past, dressed in an outfit identical to Christian's, a sassy grin tilting her wide mouth. "Is that all you ever think about, Atherton?"

"That and winning." Christian grinned back.

"How's the course look, Casanova?" Ry asked dryly.

"Interesting. I'd say that even a bit wet from last night's rain, it's going to cater to quickness, but there are three really big fences that are going to require some power to clear cleanly." He ran a hand down the stallion's neck and patted the big horse's shoulder. "He can do it. After all, it would be bad form to end his career on anything less than a win."

Bad form and bad business, Ry thought, remembering the stack of bills on his desk back home. A win today not only would pay off some debts and end Rough Cut's career on a high note, but also would leave mare owners with a positive last impression of the stallion, one that might entice them to invest in a hefty breeding fee come spring.

"Well, I think you both look too handsome to take anything less than first place," Maggie said with that familiar flirtatious tilt to her head.

"Thank you, darling," Christian said with a chuckle for Ry's disgruntled expression. "A woman of charm as well as looks."

Ry grunted and backed toward the door with Maggie in tow. "See you in the winner's circle, hotshot."

They walked out of the stables and toward the grandstand, where a good-size crowd had already gathered to watch the day's competitions. The lane was lined on both sides with food vendors and mobile tack shops. With the clean washed beauty of the fall day all around, the atmosphere was much like a country fair.

Ry glanced down at Maggie, who looked very sporty in her brown corduroy slacks and tweed jacket. He didn't want to admit how glad he'd been to see her when he came around that corner. He'd felt as if the bottom had dropped out of his stomach, almost giddy—or as close to it as he'd ever come.

"I wasn't sure you'd show up," he said evenly, carefully watching for her response.

"Why wouldn't I have come?"

His shrug was more defensive than nonchalant as he steered her toward a food stand. "You weren't exactly pleased with me when you left this morning." He ordered a pair of hot dogs with everything, fries, and a quart of soda, then turned to Maggie and asked if she wanted anything.

She rolled her eyes. As they walked away from the stand, Ry carrying a cardboard tray heaped with the food, she said, "I'm not angry with you, Rylan. I think you're wrong, and I mean to prove it to you, but I can hardly be angry with you. Besides, I promised the ladies I'd drive them here."

"What do you mean 'prove it to me'?" he asked with a suspicious look, stopping so abruptly, he nearly overturned his drink.

Walking on toward the grandstand entrance, Maggie ignored his question. She waved to Miss Emma and Mrs. Claiborne. "There they are now."

"What the hell?" Ry muttered half under his breath, temporarily stunned into forgetting his concern over Maggie's statement.

Miss Emma was dressed in blue jeans and a leather jacket. She looked like a geriatric motorcycle mama. But it was the other Darlington sister that drew Ry's attention. A wide-brimmed red straw hat shading her delicate complexion, Mrs. Claiborne stood with Junior in her arms. The little dog was sporting a tartan collar and wore a knitted red sweater against the slight chill in the air. The ensemble matched Mrs. Claiborne's sweater and plaid skirt.

"Doesn't Junior get a matching hat?" he wondered aloud. "Ouch!"

Maggie pinched his arm. "Not one smart remark, Rylan Quaid," she warned in a whisper as they drew within earshot of the ladies. "She loves that little dog to distraction. If she wants to spend her social security money on little outfits for him, that's her business."

"I'll bet you hardly recognized little Junior, did you, Mr. Quaid?" Mrs. Claiborne asked, beaming a smile at Ry.

"Oh . . ." He choked back a chuckle. Maggie glared at him. "Not hardly."

The ladies were invited to take seats with

Maggie and Ry in the Quaid Farm box where Katie and Nick had already settled in. Nick, a gourmet chef, had packed a fabulous picnic basket. He grimaced at the tray of junk food Ry settled across his knees.

"Are you going to eat that?"

"Well, I'm not going to throw it out into the arena."

Nick muttered a string of pious-sounding Italian words, shaking his handsome head. "I brought food, Ry. Did you think I wouldn't bring food?"

"He brought food on our honeymoon," Katie said, giggling.

Ry watched his brother-in-law lift dish after mouth-watering dish out of the basket. "I didn't figure you'd bring the whole damn restaurant."

"Mr. Quaid, your language," Mrs. Claiborne admonished him as she covered Junior's ears with her hands.

"Never mind his language, sister," Miss Emma said, her bright blue eyes glued on a handsome young man who was taking an equally handsome black horse through his paces over the attractive array of fences in the arena. "Take a gander at this hunk. I've decided horse shows are the perfect places to cruise for men. Just look at all these gorgeous young studs running around in those slinky, skintight breeches."

Mrs. Claiborne frowned her disapproval. "Emma, honest to Pete, you're hot as a mink."

Miss Emma laughed. "Hot as a mink in Miami!"

Nibbling on a chicken leg, Katie leaned toward Maggie with conspiracy in her gray eyes. "How goes the battle? We noticed you left the festivities early last night."

"Well—" Maggie glanced over to make sure Ry wasn't listening. He was busy wolfing down a hot dog while he looked over the program. "There was last night. . . ." The apples of her cheeks blushed a becoming shade of red. Then her mouth turned down in a frown. ". . . Then there was this morning. You wouldn't believe what he said to me."

"Yes, I would. He may have been salutatorian of his high school class, but sometimes I'd swear he doesn't have a brain in his head."

"He doesn't. I can vouch for the fact that his brain definitely resides elsewhere," she said, making a pained face. She shook her head. "But I love him anyway."

Katie's look was sympathetic. "Hang in there, friend."

Maggie laughed wearily. "Honey, by the time I get him straightened out, I'll be too exhausted to enjoy him."

"Mary Margaret," Ry said, washing his lunch down with soda, "you never answered me. What did you mean you're going to prove me wrong? What kind of game are you running now?"

"No games, sugar." She took the show program

from him and began paging through it. "We agreed this morning: no more games."

He eyed her suspiciously, looking poised to bolt away from her. No game? Maggie couldn't go ten minutes without having some kind of scam spring to life in that active little red-haired head of hers. That was one of the things he lov—found attractive about her. Now she sat there paging through the program, looking as innocent as a kitten. And as soft, and sweet, and—damn, she was wearing that perfume again!

He shifted uncomfortably on his chair, forcing his mind away from memories of the night before by analyzing the performance of the sorrel mare now in the ring. She was a nice, scopey jumper. Excellent form over her fences. She was pretty-headed, with a shiny copper-colored coat and big brown eyes. He faulted her for her short stride and for being a little too well fed, but he wouldn't have minded having her in his barn. She reminded him of Maggie. Maggie was a little too well fed, but he sure as hell didn't have any complaints about the ride she'd given him.

"Gosh almighty," he said through his teeth, settling his cardboard lunch tray more strategically across his lap. What was the matter with him? He couldn't do something as simple as look at a horse anymore without thinking of Maggie. Brows lowered, he turned his frustration on the cause. "What the hell did you mean then, if you're not up to some kind of game?"

"Nothing. You think I can't prove you wrong without making a big production of it? You think I'm going to hire a plane and have it written in the sky that I love you and know that you can love me too?"

"Hush!" he said, glancing around to see who else had heard her statement.

"I will not hush, Rylan Quaid. I love you, and I don't care who knows it."

"Jeepers cripes, Mary Margaret." His gaze went heavenward, and he waited for the sound of an airplane engine. A sky writer was exactly the kind of thing he expected from this little vixen. A hundred other equally embarrassing ideas sprang from his imagination. They were all vintage McSwain. Hell, he'd had to go and fall for a woman who had a flair for the dramatic.

Fall for? He felt his cheeks pale as he turned back toward the arena. He hadn't fallen for her. He had chosen her. He had chosen her because she suited him. Visions of the previous night swam through his head. Lord have mercy, did she suit him!

"Hell and damnation." The words were said through clenched teeth as he shifted positions and squared one leg across the other.

Maggie was oblivious to Ry's discomfort. She was busy absorbing the information in the show program, reading everything from descriptions of the various classes to advertisements for some of the participating stables. The ad for Quaid Farm showed some of the new facilities under construction. There was, of course, a photograph of Rough Cut sailing over a fence, and an invitation for horse people to attend the open house in two weeks.

Maggie had heard the event mentioned several times at the party. Now she sat back and gave it considerable thought as the grounds crew entered the ring and began tearing down jumps so the arena could be dragged and the course set up for the grand prix. The next weeks would be busy ones for Ry, but they could also provide her with the perfect opportunity to get close to him and to prove to him not only that she would fit into his life but that he would *love* having her there.

"Where do you plan to receive guests at the open house next month?" she asked.

"Huh? I don't know. I figured they'd just come on inside the main barn."

She frowned at him. "That seems rather vague. You don't want your guests to be ill at ease, do you?"

"Of course not."

"And how will you keep track of who you've spoken with, of who's seen what? Where will you serve refreshments?"

"Refreshments?"

"Haven't you decided what you're going to serve yet? Hors d'oeuvres or cookies, wine, coffee, or hot cider?"

He scowled. "Shoot, Mary Margaret, I'm trying to get buildings finished and fences painted. When am I supposed to think about reception areas and whether to have smoked pheasant or Fig Newtons?"

The Cheshire cat couldn't have come up with a better smile. "When, indeed. What you need is someone to take care of all those details for you, sugar."

"Well, I—"

Maggie turned toward her partner. "Katie, darlin', we're not so awfully busy at the store right now, are we?"

"No."

"And when was the last time I had a vacation?"

"March. You spent two weeks with your sister Lisa Jane in Boca Raton."

Maggie frowned at her friend. "That hardly counts. That was family. Surely you wouldn't object to me taking a couple of weeks off to help Rylan, would you?"

Katie smiled too sweetly. "Not at all, darlin', but if Mrs. Pruitt comes in and demands to have her bathrooms redone again, you are going to owe me in a big way."

"Deal." She swung back toward Ry. "Yes, sugar,

I can get free to help you prepare for the open house."

"Thank you," he said automatically, then sat back, bewildered. He wasn't quite sure how she'd done it, but Maggie had managed to place herself in his company for the next two weeks, had managed to make him think it had been his idea, and even had him feeling grateful. He sighed and shook his head. "You're a wonder, Mary Margaret."

"Oh, look," Maggie said, sitting up in her seat, her face glowing. "It's time for the class to start."

Maggie watched with her heart in her throat as each horse and rider negotiated the demanding course. Many failed the test in the first round. Front or hind legs knocked rails from their cups, adding costly faults to a rider's performance. A miscalculation of distance resulted in a fall of both horse and rider that had Katie Leone white. She had nearly lost her life in a similar accident.

A field of thirty was gradually whittled to eight. That was the number of horses that had made it around the arena without a single fault. Rough Cut was one of those to make the second round.

Marissa McLaughlin, riding Debutante, was the first to ride, scoring a clean round and setting a sizzling pace. Her performance held up throughout the round. Then Christian and Rough Cut entered the ring.

Maggie was so nervous, she almost fell off her

chair. She grabbed Ry's hand as soon as the whistle sounded and hung on for dear life. The stallion attacked the course, galloping to each fence with his ears pinned, and sailing over with inches to spare. Christian held nothing back, asking the big bay for everything he had. Rough Cut gave it all and then some. He cut one turn so sharply that Atherton lost a stirrup just a stride before the highest jump on the course. Maggie gasped as she saw him come up out of the saddle on the way over the fence. But the Englishman had earned his reputation as one of the top riders on the circuit. He hung on. Rough Cut sprinted for the finish line, crossing it two hundredths of a second faster than Debutante.

The occupants of the Quaid Farm box were on their feet cheering as Christian saluted the crowd with his riding crop. Mrs. Claiborne threw her red hat into the air. Miss Emma screamed and started doing the twist as Junior wagged his tail and barked. Maggie found herself engulfed in a Rylan Quaid bear hug. She was certain he was crushing each and every one of her ribs, but she was too happy for him to care.

He pulled her down to the arena with him for the awards presentation, grinning from ear to ear when Christian rode in to wild cheers from the partisan crowd.

Rough Cut was draped with a blanket proclaiming him winner of the Albemarle Cup, while the sterling silver champagne bucket was presented to Ry along with a check.

He cradled his prizes in one arm and hugged Maggie with the other.

"What do you want to do to celebrate?" he asked her. "Dinner? Champagne?"

She crooked her finger and, when he bent over, whispered the most outrageously suggestive thing she could think of. Ry's eyes instantly turned smoky with desire while his cheeks flushed. Maggie giggled and ran a finger down the side of his face. "I didn't know there were that many shades of red."

Ry laughed. "Just wait till I get you home."

Maggie batted her lashes at him. "I'd rather not." She glanced around at the grandstand full of people watching them, then turned her gaze back to Rylan. "But I don't think we have a choice."

eight

A FIRE CRACKLED in the large stone fireplace, casting the only light in the room. Warmth was the primary sensation. Warmth from the fire, from the thick soft blanket that covered her from shoulder to toe, from the solid body of the man she snuggled against, and from his arms wrapped around her. The warmth of contentment filled her. Contentment from making love, from being full of good food and good wine, from knowing this was all real instead of a dream.

Nuzzling her cheek against Ry's chest, Maggie sighed and smiled. After Rough Cut's victory there had been champagne back in the stables for family, friends, and syndicate investors. From there the party had moved to Briarwood, to Nick's restaurant, where they had celebrated with a fabulous dinner. Not that she was antisocial or anything, but Maggie's favorite part had been the private celebration she and Ry had shared.

The sterling champagne bucket that had been awarded to them that afternoon now sat on the coffee table with a nearly empty bottle of wine sticking up out of it. The firelight glowed on the fine engraving that marked the piece as the Albemarle Cup. Tomorrow it would take its place among the hundreds of other trophies on one of the shelves that lined the walls of the large room. Tonight it was being included in the celebration. Just as Maggie was being included.

A particularly feline smile turned her lips. She loved the way Ry was including her in the celebration.

She stretched, arching her body against his, glorying in his strength and hardness. He had a magnificent body. Her hands couldn't resist exploring it, the hills and valleys of muscles and their lines of delineation. Lazily raising her head to watch, she began at his wide, wide shoulders and moved slowly downward, over his thickset chest. She ran her thumb down over the rippling planes of his stomach, changing course abruptly when he stiffened and sucked in his breath. Tossing the red blanket back, she stared at the pure male beauty of him as her hand traced over his hip, then started up his other heavily muscled thigh.

"So handsome," she whispered, watching her fingertips trail back up his rib cage and nestle into the curling dark hair that carpeted his chest. She let her gaze continue up to his face. He was watching her intently. "I love your body. . . ." She leaned down to brush a kiss across his mouth. ". . . the way it looks . . ." Her eyes locked with his as her hand slid back down. ". . . the way it works . . ."

Ry tried to force himself to lie still while she explored. He had always considered himself a man of tremendous self-control. Until Maggie. Even now, when they had already spent a night together and had already made love once, his blood was jumping in his veins. The need, the desire had not been slaked in the least. In fact, the more he had of her, the more he wanted. In that respect, she was wreaking havoc on his famous plan, but he couldn't complain when she touched him, when she looked at him as though he was the one and only thing in the world she wanted.

Before she could drive him completely over the

brink and into madness, he turned the tables on her, rolling her onto her back. He propped himself up on one elbow. His other hand ran gently down from her shoulder to cup her full breast with its wide dusky center and pouting nipple, down the sweeping curve to her narrow waist, and over the rounded flare of her hip.

"So feminine . . . soft . . . pretty . . ."

Maggie's heart fluttered. Words like that were rare from him. She soaked them up and felt each one of them blossom inside her.

"I like this little swell right here," he said, stroking just below her navel.

"What a kind euphemism for fat," she said, chuckling softly. "You'll never see this body in a fashion magazine."

He kissed his way down to the spot. "I never was one for those long, skinny women."

"Hallelujah." Her breath grew shorter as his kisses became longer and more passionate and slipped lower than the area he had been admiring. His lips nibbled their way back up her hip, paused at her breast, then found their way back to her mouth.

"Did the ladies give you any trouble about coming to stay here with me?" he asked, rolling onto his back and snuggling Maggie to his side once again.

"No. Mrs. Claiborne thinks the world of you—"

"Except for my language."

"—and Miss Emma told me she was envious enough to make it a mortal sin."

Ry laughed. "They're something else, those two."

Maggie smiled fondly. "They're wonderful. I love them like family. Besides, they agreed with me. They both said a social function like this open house needs a woman's supervision."

He snorted. "With the possible exception of car maintenance, women think everything needs a woman's supervision."

"I didn't hear you complaining about my supervision earlier this evening."

"Oh, that was supervising, was it? I could have sworn that was moaning and sighing in wanton abandon."

"Wanton abandon!" She raised up and loomed over him, brown eyes sparkling with reflected light from the fire. "Huh! I'll give you wanton abandon, mister."

Ry's gaze fastened on the sway of her breasts no more than a hair's breadth from his chest. "Hallelujah."

They made love slowly. Ry let Maggie take the lead until his fragile hold on control slipped. Then Maggie wrapped her arms around him and hung on, arching up to meet his deep hard thrusts until fulfillment came, as hot and brilliant as the shower of sparks that burst upward from the fire in the grate.

Ry held himself deep inside her, gasping as he absorbed shock wave after shock wave of her pleasure. Gradually the intensity decreased. Tenderly he brushed her hair back from her face and kissed her sweet red lips. "Ah, Maggie . . . oh, honey . . . I . . ."

If there had been more words, they were stubbornly lodged in his throat. No, he thought as he gazed down at her, it felt more as if they were lodged in his heart. He wanted to tell her . . . something. That he cared, cared deeply. That he wanted to make her happy. That . . . ah, hell, nothing seemed adequate.

"I love you, Ry," she whispered, watching him struggle with feelings he didn't seem to understand.

His dark brows pulled together in concern over stormy eyes the color of Spanish moss. "Maggie—"

She lifted a hand and pressed her fingers to his lips. "Let me say it. I love you. I'm going to keep on saying it, because it's what I feel."

And because, maybe, if she kept on saying it, someday soon he would be able to believe in that love and say those same words to her.

Maggie didn't consider it a plan really. Everything she did was open and aboveboard. She wanted to give Ry a taste of the kind of life they could have together. There was certainly nothing devious in that. And it wasn't as if she hadn't told him that was what she was going to do. So if she told him at unexpected times that she loved him, if she showed up in his office with lunch and wearing nothing but a sexy negligee under her coat, he couldn't say he hadn't been forewarned.

What she spent most of her time doing, however, was working. There were a million tiny details to putting on an open house. Ry had been too busy to see to any of them. While he and his crew worked on the buildings and fences, she took care of ordering the food, calling a sign maker, lining up workers, contacting the greenhouse for bouquets. While Ry and Christian instructed grooms to clean every piece of tack and brush every horse on the place until the shine on their coats was blinding, Maggie was overseer to the small army of help rented to scrub and polish Ry's office as well as the lounge that looked out on the indoor riding arena.

Both those rooms underwent a whirlwind redecoration. Braided rugs were spread across the floors, tasteful, comfortable chairs replaced the mismatched wobbly-legged ones. Patchwork pillows and a quilt done in the royal blue and gray that were the Quaid Farm colors added a homeyness to the lounge. Ry's office was decorated with hunting prints. As a special present, Maggie bought him an oversize leather-covered desk chair with brass nailhead trim. His desk was cleaned and oiled, the cheap old blotter replaced with one that matched his chair. His paperwork was neatly tucked into the new set of stack trays on the corner of his desk.

When she could spare five or ten minutes, Maggie spent them with the orphaned foal, grooming him or just petting him and talking to him. She managed to get in one riding lesson with Christian. He patiently assured her she wasn't hopeless, but it was plain no one on the U.S. equestrian team was in any danger of losing his spot.

On top of this mountain of work, she also saw to Ry's meals, his house, his needs. When he was thirsty from working out under the sun, she was there with a glass of lemonade. When he came in at the end of a long day feeling as if he'd "been rode hard and put away wet," she saw to it he had a hot shower, a hot meal, and a long, loving massage.

Was she making any headway? she wondered at the end of day six. It was hard to say. Ry seemed to genuinely appreciate her help with the arrangements. He ate the food she cooked and didn't hesitate to reach for her when they went to bed at night. But he didn't seem any closer to telling her he loved her.

He told her he wanted her. He told her he needed her. He told her she was a godsend. But he never said the words she'd vowed she had to hear before she would marry him.

Maybe she was being too stubborn. It could take Ry years to express those feelings. Why did she have to hear them? If she knew he felt them, wasn't that enough?

No, that wasn't enough. It wasn't so much that she had to hear him say he could love. What she really wanted was for him to know he had that wealth of love inside him. It was a wonderful feeling to love someone, to revel in that love, to nurture it and feel it grow. If she gave in now, he might never take that chance with his heart, and he would go on cheating himself, cheating them both.

She sighed as she bent to pull on her riding boots. *Patience, Maggie, patience.* He would come around. Sooner or later. Maybe something would happen to open the door to his heart. Maybe one of these times when she told him she loved him, it would sink into that hunk of titanium he called a skull.

Straightening, she looked at herself in the front hall mirror and made a face. Sure, she looked okay in her rust breeches and oatmeal-colored sweater, with tortoiseshell barrettes in her hair. By the time her lesson was over, her bob would have bounced itself up into a Bozo-the-Clown look. With any luck she would run into Ry before she rode and not after.

• • •

Ry sank down to the welcoming softness of his new desk chair. The day had been unbelievably long. Only half the equipment he'd ordered for the new veterinarian facilities in the breeding shed had been delivered. The rest, the delivery man had informed him, was on back-order. Dammit, when a man shelled out top money for top equipment he expected it to be delivered on time. Then one of his many mongrel dogs had spooked a young horse he'd just picked up at an auction. The filly had crashed through a section of new board fence and toppled three five-gallon buckets of paint.

There had been a dozen other small irritations, mostly in the form of bills. He had never been very fond of parting with his money. This open house was costing more than he had expected. So were the renovations to the farm. He had to keep reminding himself that while all the cash was flowing out this week, it would be flowing in next. Next week the syndication would be finalized, the investors would pay him. Then, next spring, when they were booked up with visiting mares and hauling money to the bank by the wheelbarrow, he would look back on these two weeks and laugh.

Tonight he wasn't laughing. He had a headache the size of Rhode Island. He needed a shower, a meal, a glass of good white wine, and quiet. What he didn't need was Maggie coming to him with another piddling problem to solve or a color swatch to approve or a receipt to sign. And if she told him one more time that she was in love with him . . .

What, jerk? a little voice inside his throbbing head asked. *What will you do, yell at her? Throw her off the place? Go ahead, show her just how unlovable you really are.*

"Oh, hell," he muttered, rubbing a hand across his forehead.

Maggie was only trying to help. She'd done a hell of a job shaping up the areas where the guests would be received and entertained. Arrangements for food and drink had been taken care of. If those details had been left up to him, the way his schedule was running, he would have ended up serving the guests stale crackers and peanut butter out of his kitchen. He hadn't even had time to check on Rough Cut since they'd brought him home, even though he'd been aching to take the stallion out for a little exercise. Maggie had been a big help.

So what was his problem? Why was he so ready to bite the poor woman's head off?

Because he was tired. Because he was feeling edgy. She wanted something from him he couldn't give her. She wanted to give him something he would sooner not accept. And the whole business was forcing him to look into a part of himself he would rather have left alone—old feelings, old hurts, old fears.

"Let sleeping dogs lie, Maggie," he said under his breath.

He swung his chair around to face his desk, but when he went to put his feet in the cubby hole they were met with an outraged bark. Ry slid out of the chair and ducked under the desk, groaning at the sight that greeted him.

"Shasta, you can't keep your puppies under here."

The golden retriever gave him a pleading look. Her brood lay curled up next to her belly, sound asleep. She had obviously carried them one by one out of the new kennel Ry had moved her to and stowed them under his desk. Carefully, he scooped up two puppies in each hand and carried them around to the new braided rug in front of his desk. Shasta followed him, whining a protest. He crawled half under the desk again to scoop out more puppies.

"This is an interesting view." Maggie's voice floated in from the doorway.

Ry jerked his head up, smacking it into the underside of the desk. Swear words rolled out from under the sturdy piece of furniture like a cloud of acrid smoke.

"Sugar, such language." Maggie tsk-tsked, coming to the desk to help him. She bent over and accepted the pair of taffy-colored pups he handed out. "And in front of the babies."

"Dammit, Mary Margaret, you hadn't ought to sneak up on a man like that."

"I'm sorry." She raised on tiptoe to kiss his scowling mouth when he stood up with a puppy in each hand. "What are these little darlin's doing in here?"

Ry turned his dour look on Shasta. The dog whined and looked woebegone, but thumped her shaggy tail hopefully. "The little mother decided she didn't like the new accommodations. Between her and that flea-bitten pack of rat hounds outside, I swear, I'm gonna lose my mind. I oughta ship the lot of them to the pound."

"But you won't," Maggie said softly, snuggling the puppies to her chest, her heart aching with love for Ry.

Ry frowned at the puppies in his hands. He walked around the desk and set them on the rug beside Shasta. "No, I won't. Lord only knows why not."

"I'm in on the secret, too, sugar." Maggie reunited mother and munchkins, then stood and sent Ry a knowing smile. "It's because you're sweet and good and have a soft spot for helpless creatures that need love."

He actually felt it snap. The hair-thin thread that had been holding his temper in check frayed and broke. He wheeled on Maggie. "Jeepers cripes, Mary Margaret, do you have to make a federal case out of it? I show a little common decency to a few stray animals, and you make me out to be Saint Francis of Assisi."

Maggie jammed her hands on her hips. "I don't see why you have such a problem acknowledging the fact that you give love to these animals."

"I don't give . . . that. I feed them and house them, that's all."

"Lord have mercy, you can't even say it!" Her laugh was one born of frustration, not humor. "Love. Love, Rylan. It's the only four-letter word not in regular use in your vocabulary! Why can't you admit you have it and you give it?"

"And why do you have to be so bloody stubborn, insisting that I give something that I don't have in me?"

"Stubborn!" she shouted. "*You're* calling *me* stubborn? Sugar, you wrote the book on it! You are the original immovable object. I could just as well go beat my head against a stone wall as try to talk sense into you."

"Then why don't you!" he shouted back, swinging an arm toward the open door. "I sure as hell don't need you hanging around here, sticking your nose in where it doesn't belong."

Tears sprang to her eyes as quickly as if he had slapped her, but Maggie spun on her heel and stormed out of the room before Ry could see them. It was bad enough she'd let him have the last word, she wasn't about to let him see how badly those words had hurt.

Her step faltered as she continued down the aisle of the barn, and she realized with no small amount of shame that she had been hoping he would come after her. She had been hoping he would spin her around and scoop her up into his arms and kiss her and apologize.

"Dream on, darlin'," she muttered bitterly, blinking back scalding tears, "it's what you do best."

Her booted feet pounded down the cement alleyway. She kept her head up and choked back the lump in her throat as she passed two grooms.

"Killer's all ready for your lesson, Miz McSwain," called one.

Maggie hiccupped and thanked him without breaking stride. Without really thinking about what she was doing, she went to the end stall. The brown gelding stood dozing, flipping his lips. He was indeed tacked up, saddled and bridled. With little half sobs escaping her throat, she led the horse out the end of the barn, stood on a wooden block to mount, then turned him toward the hills and kicked him into a trot.

The tears flowed freely as soon as she was away from the stables. They blurred her vision and streamed down her cheeks. She paid no attention at all to where she was going, letting Killer choose his own path. She merely hung on and cried her heart out.

"Damn you, Rylan Quaid," she said, sobbing. "Damn me for loving you."

It wasn't fair. She'd worked so hard. Not just

helping with the preparations, but with trying to help Ry break down the walls he'd built around his heart.

"Did it ever occur to you that maybe he didn't build them up with the intention of letting you tear them down, Maggie?" she asked herself in a strangled voice.

Maybe what she had to realize was that Ry was right. Maybe he wasn't capable of loving her. Maybe she had to face up to the possibility that she couldn't make him love her. Love came naturally or not at all. And just because he was the man of her dreams, just because she'd fallen in love with him all those years ago, didn't mean he had to feel the same depth of emotion.

As long as she was facing facts, she had to admit that the man she'd fallen in love with originally had been nothing more than a figment of her imagination. She'd discovered that when she had finally started spending time with Ry. He wasn't the man who swept her around ballrooms and wrote poetry. He was a man who was tough but tender, who could have won a world champion-ship for scowling but who took in any helpless creature that needed him. She'd seen he was a man who didn't trust emotions, who held a part of himself back from others. And she'd fallen in love with him anyway.

"So, it's your own darn fault, McSwain," she said, reaching up to swipe away some of the tears that clung to her lashes. "You deserve whatever happens to you."

At that instant a deer bounded out from behind some brush and shot across the path directly in front of a very startled Killer. Wild-eyed, the gelding executed a hasty half pirouette and dashed out from under his rider.

Maggie didn't even have time to realize what had happened before she hit the ground and everything went black.

"Aw, hell, why did I have to be such a bastard?" Ry asked himself aloud. He sat behind his desk, his elbows on the blotter, his head cradled in his hands.

He hadn't meant to tear into her like that. He had intended to thank her for the work she'd done on his office. Well, he'd blown that royally. Instead of thanking her, he'd practically thrown all her hard work back in her face.

She'd been crying when she'd stormed out. He hadn't seen the tears, but he'd heard the jerky intake of breath, he'd seen the way she set her shoulders, he'd heard her hiccup. Damn. It tore him up inside to know he'd made her cry.

It had been a long, hard day. He was tired. He was feeling edgy and crowded by Maggie's continual declarations of love. That still didn't excuse what he'd done. He'd have to go find her and apologize. Hopefully she would forgive him.

Maybe when he went into town tomorrow he could stop by Leebright's Jewelry Store and pick her up a little something just to make her feel better.

And to soothe your own miserable conscience, he told himself.

Why did life have to be so doggone complicated?

Two brisk knocks sounded on the office door before it swung open. Christian stepped inside, his usual smile in place. "I came to fetch Maggie for her lesson."

"She's not here," Ry mumbled.

"She's not here?" Atherton glanced around the newly refurbished room. His smile faded to a frown. "She's not here."

"Brilliant deduction, Sherlock," Ry said sarcastically.

Christian was unperturbed. "Ah, a lover's quarrel. Well, perhaps she can channel her anger into something productive. She needs to be more aggressive as a rider anyway. Where did she go?"

"I don't know. Maybe she went up to the house. Maybe she left. Maybe she went to get a gun so she can blow my stupid head off."

"Oh, quit feeling sorry for yourself. Feel sorry for me. I've been cooling my heels for the last ten minutes waiting for her to show up in the arena."

"Hey, Marlin," Ry called to the groom passing the open office door.

The young man stuck his dark head in. "Yes, sir?"

"Have you seen Miss McSwain in the last half hour or so?"

"Yes, sir. She took Killer out about that long ago."

Ry's brows knitted in concern. "Took him out where?"

"I couldn't say for sure. I was grooming Specialty when she stomp—er—walked past. She went down to Killer's stall and took him out the end of the barn. I reckon she rode up into the woods."

Ry let loose a stream of words that could have turned the air blue as he launched himself out of his chair. Maggie wasn't a good enough rider to head into the woods on her own. She didn't know her way around. She could barely stay on the blasted horse just trotting around the arena.

Young Marlin turned gray at his boss's outburst. His Adam's apple bobbed nervously in his throat.

"Fool woman! She's gonna get herself lost up there—or worse—and it's damn near dark." Ry poked a rigid index finger at the groom. "I want a horse saddled, and if it's not ready in five minutes, I'll have your rear on a platter."

"Yessir!"

Exactly five minutes later Ry was on horseback, galloping away from the farm and toward the wooded hills. As his horse ate up the distance with long, smooth strides, he tried to reassure himself with the knowledge that Maggie was on the gentlest horse he owned. But fear still churned in his belly. Even gentle horses could be startled into irrational behavior. If Maggie hadn't checked her equipment—of course she wouldn't have, given the state of mind she'd been in—her girth might have been loose. She had no natural sense of balance. If the saddle slipped, she'd be under her horse's belly in the blink of an eye. There were any number of ways she could get hurt.

And it was all his fault. That terrible knowledge pressed down on him like a black iron weight. He had lashed out at her, hurt her, driven her to run away. He wouldn't be able to live with himself if anything had happened to her. And he knew with a sudden chilling clarity that his life would be a desolate place if he had to live without her. Living without Maggie would be like living without half of himself. He needed her. He loved her.

The realization brought on a fresh surge of fear. He loved her, yet he'd driven her to do something as stupid as taking off on a horse when she could barely stay astride. If she were hurt, he'd never forgive himself. If she were—

He deliberately cut the thought off before he could complete it and concentrated instead on where she might have gone. She had been riding in the woods only once, so it stood to reason she would follow the same path. If she remembered what path that was. With no better idea, Ry turned his horse, standing in the irons as the big gray bounded up the hill, following the old logging trail.

What daylight was left did not make it through the thick canopy of trees. It was difficult for a human to see. So it was Killer's nicker of recognition for his stablemate that first alerted Ry he was on the right track. A second later, the shape of the horse materialized, his outline suddenly becoming distinguishable from the shapes of trees and bushes.

Ry's heartbeat doubled. The saddle was empty. Then, for only the second time in his life, he felt the choking fingers of true panic close around his throat. Twenty feet beyond the brown gelding a still figure lay flat on the bed of leaves that covered the trail.

"Maggie!" Ry shouted, dismounting before his horse could pull up. He hit the ground running and fell on his knees beside the unconscious body of the woman he loved. His hands were shaking as he reached down to touch her face. She was as pale as an ivory cameo, and seemed as lifeless. Terrified, Ry drew two fingers down the side of her throat trying to find her pulse. "Maggie, sweetheart. Oh, baby, please don't be dead. I love you so much."

His fingertips finally settled on the proper spot and Ry heaved a sigh at the feel of her blood pumping through the pulse point. Still rattled, he tried to school his brain to the coolheaded discipline he'd always known, but as had happened when he'd seen his sister go down on a jump course five years before, emotions kept snatching at his control. He'd found her pulse, but was it strong enough, didn't it seem too slow? He wanted to gather her up in his arms and hold her, but he knew better than to move someone who had taken a fall and might possibly have suffered a neck or back injury.

Swallowing the knot in his throat, he began an examination with his eyes and hands, starting with her head, looking for blood. He cursed the darkness that prevented him from seeing well. If she were bleeding he would feel the sticky substance on his hands, but bruises and swelling would be almost impossible to distinguish in the fading light.

"Maggie, honey, can you hear me? I'm so sorry I hurt you. I didn't mean what I said back there. I want you on the farm. I love you."

"You would have to be too blasted hardheaded to admit it until it was too late," she mumbled weakly, struggling to clear her head of the thick fog that had blacked everything else out.

Ry bent over her, his trembling hands smoothing back her hair. "Honey? Are you all right?"

She groaned. "What kind of damn fool question is that?"

"Don't try to sit up yet," he said, gently holding her down when she tried to raise her head. "Open your eyes and take a couple of good deep breaths if you can. Tell me where it hurts, sweetheart."

"All over a little bit, but I think I'm all right." At least everything seemed to be in working order, she thought, moving her arms and legs just enough to reassure herself. Her heart, in particular, was working very well. It had started pounding the instant she had heard Ry's words. "I got the wind knocked out of me, that's all." Her fingers scratched back through her hair, and she winced at the little knob that had raised up on the back of her skull. "I guess I hit my head too."

Ry tried in vain to check her pupils. It simply was too dark to see the black dots encircled by the dark brown of her irises. "How many fingers am I holding up?"

"Two."

"Good. I'm going to move my finger from side to side. Don't move your head, just follow it with your eyes."

After she'd done as he asked, relieving his fear that she might have suffered a concussion, Maggie lifted herself up on her elbows and gave him a rueful smile. "Guess I shouldn't have come up here by myself. I was so hurt—"

"Hush, sweetheart. Don't talk right now, just let me hold you." His breath was still rushing in and out of his lungs and his arms were still quivering as he wrapped them around her. "Lord, Mary Margaret, I swear you scared ten years off my life."

"I'm sorry—"

"No. I'm sorry." His lips brushed her hair when he spoke. He breathed in the scent of shampoo and earth and dried leaves. Nothing had ever smelled so wonderful. "When I was riding up here, all I could think about was what terrible things could have happened to you and that it would have been my fault. I was sick at the thought that I might lose you when I'd finally looked past the nose on my face and seen that I was in love with you. When I saw you lying here, I thought I was gonna die."

Maggie hugged him as hard as she could, considering she was still shaken up, both from the fall and from finally hearing him tell her that what she had dreamed of all these years had finally come true. "I'm all right, sugar. I'm fine. You don't have to worry anymore."

He drew back and gave her a hard look. "Are you sure? No broken bones or anything?"

"I don't think so," she said shaking her head. A mischievous smile pulled at the corners of her mouth. She tilted her head and said, "I suppose it wouldn't hurt to have you check me over for broken bones. You know, run those big strong hands of yours all over me. Just in case."

It was amazing how something as subtle as the tone of her voice could make his blood turn thick in his veins. When the words spilled off her lips as smooth and sweet as warm clover honey, everything male in him snapped to attention. He smiled down at her. She looked like some kind of woodland nymph with leaves clinging to her sweater, and her hair a wild cloud around her head.

"Are you suggesting what I think you're suggesting?"

She merely continued staring up at him with wide, dark eyes.

He stared back, the sudden sexual intensity sobering his expression. "It's getting cold."

"Then you'll have to warm us up." She reached out and ran her fingertips inside the waistband of his jeans, gently pulling him closer. "Won't you, sugar?"

His voice dropped to a rough whisper. "We're in the middle of the woods."

"And you've just told me something I've been waiting my whole life to hear." All teasing was gone from her expression now. She spoke what was in her heart. "I love you, Ry. You've just told me you love me. Please let's celebrate that."

Their lips met, softly, sweetly, as Ry's fingers caught the edge of Maggie's sweater. She took his tongue into her mouth, sucking gently, inviting him to explore and to claim while her fingers dealt with the snaps on his denim shirt.

The chill of a fall night settled in around them,

but they were encased in a heat that was of their own making. Naked, they stretched out together with Ry's shirt as a blanket over the bed of soft, crunching leaves.

She lay on her back, open to him, inviting him. He stayed on his knees a moment longer, looking down at her. She was so lovely, so womanly, and she was his. They had miraculously arrived at the same plane of awareness. At least for this moment their lives were entwined heart and soul. That was indeed something worth celebrating. It was something he had never known before, something he had never expected to know, something he knew would never happen again. What a precious gift it was to have this time with Maggie.

Slowly he bent and kissed each dusky, pebble-hard nipple. He kissed the pulse point in the base of her throat before moving back to her lips. His body stretched out alongside hers, the heat of his arousal branding her hip as he pressed against her. His hand stroked down through the tangle of fiery curls that hid her femininity, big rough fingers gently parting the soft petals that sheltered her sweetest secrets.

"Ah, Maggie," he whispered.

She lifted her hips in the rhythm his hand set, moaning as he brought her to the edge of ecstasy but refused to take her over. She whispered his name, the sound rich with a complex mix of emotions—love, need, desire, devotion. They were emotions that tightened together, concentrating in one vulnerable, highly sensitive spot his fingertips touched each time he reached deep inside her.

His lips nuzzled through her hair to the shell of her ear. "Sweet Maggie. You're so hot, so wet. I want you so badly, sometimes I think I'll go crazy from it."

"I want you, Ry," she murmured, trying to pull his body across hers. "Please."

"I . . . love . . . you," he said, the words sounding rusty from lack of use. He cleared his throat and tried again. "I love you, Maggie."

Tears of joy glistened in her eyes. This time when she reached for him he went to her. He mounted her in one smooth swift move, filling her heat with his hardness. Her sweet, sharp cry soared through the gathering night, mingling with the other calls of nature, of life.

They moved together, straining toward the same goal—the perfect physical expression of what was in their hearts. And when the moment came, it was golden.

They rode back to the farm together on Ry's horse. Sitting sidesaddle across the pommel wasn't the most comfortable position Maggie had ever been in, but she uttered not one complaint. Ry was giving full rein to his protective instincts. He didn't want her more than an arm's length away from him. In fact, he seemed to want her plastered to his side like a Siamese twin. There was no way on earth he was going to let her ride her own horse back.

That was okay by her. Snuggling into Ry's solid warmth was much more appealing than perching herself on top of that four-legged ballet star. All the little aches her fall had won her throbbed a bit harder at the thought of riding again.

"You're staying in the arena after this, unless I'm with you," Ry dictated. "And you're buying a hard hat tomorrow."

"And a suit of armor," she joked.

It was on the tip of her tongue to say maybe she wasn't cut out to be an equestrian, that maybe she should quit while she was behind. But she didn't say it, and she banished the idea from her mind. She didn't want Ry to think she was a quitter. She wanted to please him, to make him proud of her. When they got back to the stables she was going to find Christian and set up another lesson. Then she was going to go to the house and soak in a hot bath for the next three days.

Ry hugged her closer, resisting the urge to forbid her to ride again. He wanted her safe. He reminded himself she was safe, and that the best way to keep her safe, if she was going to live on a horse farm, was to educate her. He couldn't keep her wrapped in cotton for all of their married lives.

Married life. He smiled and pressed a kiss into

her hair. There was nothing to keep them from getting married now. The future was nothing but blue skies. He had Maggie, safe and warm in his arms. The thought of being in love with her still frightened him a little, but he tried to ignore the feeling. Why should it frighten him when he was assured of having her with him? In another week the syndication of Rough Cut would be complete, the money would officially change hands, and he would be able to give Maggie the kind of life-style financial security allowed, the lifestyle an admiral's daughter expected.

They rode down out of the woods at a leisurely pace, enjoying the moon-silvered scenery and each other. All too soon, the white buildings of the farm came into view, their windows all glowing with amber light. They were fifty yards away from the main barn when Marlin, the young groom, came tearing out to meet them, his face grim.

"Mr. Quaid, come quick! It's Rough Cut!"

nine

"WHAT'S HAPPENED?" Ry asked anxiously as he handed Maggie down. He dismounted and handed the reins of both his horse and Killer to the nervous groom.

"He's sick, sir, real sick. Mr. Atherton already called Dr. Maclay."

Ry's strides lengthened as he headed for the stable, concern plain on his face. Maggie jogged to keep up with him.

"What can I do to help?"

"Run down to the dispensary, get that big leather doctor's bag that sits on the counter, and meet me at Cutter's stall."

She did as she was told, as quickly as possible, running down the aisle of the barn, dodging stray dogs and biting her lip against the pain pounding in her temples from her fall. In the dispensary she pulled the black bag off the counter and was certain she had separated her shoulder when the thing nearly pulled her to the floor. Struggling, she heaved it up into both arms and charged out of the room, nearly tripping over a coonhound as she ran toward Rough Cut's stall.

What did they do with sick horses? she wondered. Would he be taken to an animal hospital? The only thing she could think of was that they shot horses with broken legs. Cutter wasn't injured, he was sick. Surely there was something a vet could do to save him. There had to be; this horse was Ry's pride and his livelihood. Maggie offered up a hasty, breathless prayer for the big stallion.

When she rounded the corner she was met with an unusually serious look from Christian Atherton. The stall door was rolled back and Ry and two grooms were in with Rough Cut, trying to assess the situation. The horse was in obvious pain. Sweat darkened his copper coat; he pawed the floor of his stall, then groaned and kicked at his belly with a hind leg. A groom stood on either side of his head, each with one hand firmly holding his halter and one stroking his neck. Ry spoke in a low, soothing tone of voice as he ran a hand over the stallion's side. Apparently angry with his condition, the horse pinned his ears and kicked back savagely. The sound of a steel-shod hoof connecting with the wood lining of the stall rang out like a gunshot.

"What's wrong with him?" Maggie asked, eyes round with fear at the stallion's behavior. She practically flung the medical bag in to Rylan.

"Not sure yet," he murmured as he opened the bag.

Ry shut everything else out of his mind—the syndication, Maggie and concentrated on examining the horse. One by one, he filed the symptoms into his mind to be evaluated. Pulse: fifty-one beats per minute. Fast and thready with irregular peaks. Rough Cut's normal resting rate was about thirty-eight strong, steady beats per minute. With a stethoscope he listened to the stallion's stomach, checking for normal digestive track sounds, finding instead much louder noises.

"Looks like colic, but there's something here that doesn't fit," Ry commented, shaking down a thermometer.

He tried to ignore his feeling of foreboding and wished he hadn't voiced his uncertainty. Colic was a common enough affliction, one that was relatively easy to deal with. It probably was what they were looking at. Why borrow trouble thinking they were faced with a more formidable problem?

Maybe because way in the back of his mind he had been waiting for the other shoe to fall. Things had been going his way. He was on the verge of having everything he wanted. Maybe it was just too good to be true.

And maybe he was being paranoid in the extreme, he thought, cursing his suddenly superstitious nature.

"What's colic?" Maggie asked Christian. "Is it fatal?"

"It's the equine equivalent of a bellyache, only more serious." He glanced from the horse to Maggie and back. "Yes, it can be fatal if it's not treated properly."

Maggie frowned. "What do we do?"

A violent curse erupted from Ry, drawing everyone's immediate attention. "He's got a temperature of a hundred and five. Hasn't anyone been taking care of this animal? His temperature couldn't jump six points overnight."

"Yes, sir," Bobby said. "I been looking after him." The groom paused and swallowed hard. "He's been a little off his feed, but no more than he usually is when y'all bring him home from a show. He always goes off a bit for a day or two. He hasn't seemed sick."

"Well, he's sure as hell sick now, and I don't like the look of it at all." He pulled a fresh hypodermic needle from his bag and inserted it into a bottle of clear fluid.

"What are you giving him?" Maggie bit her lip. Damnation, the sight of needles made her queasy. She braced a hand against the door frame of the stall and swallowed hard.

"Something to ease the pain. It'll also fight the fever. And we'll give him a mild tranquilizer to try to relax him so he's not as aware of his misery, the poor fella."

She wondered if they could get Ry to take a little bit of that tranquilizer. He winced every time Rough Cut groaned. The lines of sudden strain that creased across his forehead and around his mouth made him look ten years older. Maggie wanted to go to him and put her arms around him, to say something reassuring, but she knew he had work to do. He would feel better doing his best to make Rough Cut comfortable until the vet arrived.

The shot given, Ry turned back toward his medical bag. "Let's get him out of the stall and walk him a bit—"

"Rylan, look out!" Maggie shouted. She grabbed his arm and yanked, pulling him off balance and out of the way just as Rough Cut went down like a ton of bricks. The horse's legs thrashed. He stretched his neck out and bared his teeth as air hissed in and out of his flared nostrils.

Heart pounding, Maggie hugged Ry close, knowing the same kind of knee-weakening relief he had felt when he'd learned she hadn't been seriously injured in her fall from Killer. Ry gave her a quick, hard squeeze, then turned back to the horse. Quickly he checked the animal's vital signs again, his own heart pounding in his chest.

Where was the damn vet? he wondered. Why did this kind of thing invariably happen to the best horse in the barn? Why did it have to happen at all? He had wanted to spend the evening with Maggie, snuggling together on the couch, planning their wedding. With Rough Cut so desperately ill, that idea was going to have to be put on hold indefinitely.

When he left the stall he went to Maggie with a look of apology and regret. With his hands cupping her shoulders, he sighed heavily. "Go on up to the house, honey. We're in for a long night out here."

Maggie's reaction to that was immediate and genuine. "No! I will not go sit in the house like some useless lump. I'm going to be a part of this farm too, Rylan Quaid. Don't you dare try to shut me out of this. That horse is my meal ticket too, you know. I'll darn well help when he's sick."

"All right, all right." He held a hand up to cut

202

her off. There was no time for argument now. "You and Christian run to the tack room. Bring back leg wraps, a wool blanket, and all the towels we've got."

She hopped up and kissed his cheek, uttering a quick thank-you before she tore off after the trainer. She was going to become Rylan's wife. That meant becoming his partner in every way —in his barn as well as in his bed, in sickness and health, in good times and bad. She hoped it wasn't an omen of any kind that they were starting out with the worst aspects of those vows.

Dr. Maclay was a short, sturdy man dressed in a serviceable dark blue jumpsuit. He was soft-spoken and serious-faced. His gray hairs out-numbered the brown hairs three to one. He was a man Ry had great respect for, but what he was saying now, as they stood outside Rough Cut's stall, was something Ry didn't want to hear and wouldn't believe.

"Ry, I'll bet every nickel in my retirement fund we're looking at Potomac horse fever."

"That's impossible! Every horse on the place was vaccinated." Ry's heart thudded in his chest at the slim possibility he was wrong. They couldn't have missed vaccinating the most important animal on the farm. It simply wasn't possible.

The vet shook his head. "This horse couldn't have been. He's showing every single symptom. I can't tell you how he got it or where he got it, but he's got it."

"But he can't—"

Maclay cut him off with a stern look. "You don't want him to have it, and I don't blame you, but it's what we're dealing with, son, so you'd better accept it. We've got our work cut out to save this horse's life."

Maggie shivered at the ominous tone of the veterinarian's voice and at the grim expressions of the men around her. She tugged at Christian's coat sleeve and whispered, "What's Potomac fever?"

His eyes were as bleak as a sunless winter day. He never took them off the horse that had carried him to the top of the show-jumping world. "Bad news, luv. Very bad news."

The vigil began. In addition to the medication Ry had given the horse, Dr. Maclay administered antibiotics and antihistamines. Fluids were pumped into him intravenously. The grooms bandaged his legs to prevent him from hurting himself when the pain caused him to thrash about. Maggie pitched in, helping Ry and Christian as they worked continuously to try to bring down the horse's fever. She soaked towels in cold water then handed them to the men, who bathed Rough Cut with them.

It was after midnight when she finally obeyed Ry's order to go to the house. She trudged up the porch steps, her body aching from the fall she'd taken, her arms and shoulders sore and tired from wringing out towels. Moaning, she sank down onto the bentwood rocker and struggled with her boots, letting one then the other thud to the floor of the porch. A hot shower and a soft bed had never sounded so good, she thought, leaning back in the chair.

Her gaze fell on the main barn, the only building still lit up. Ry wouldn't see a hot shower or a bed until this was over. It would be a minor miracle if they got him to leave Rough Cut's stall for more than a few minutes. He would tell everyone else to take periodic breaks, but he would never give himself one. He was the one who had read book after book about veterinary science. Taking care of animals was his whole life, even though he had never been given the chance to earn his degree. He would stay with Rough Cut night and day, seeing to the horse's every need.

But who would see to Rylan?

"That's your job, Mary Margaret," Maggie said, running her hands back through her hair, dislodging bits of twigs and dried leaves. "You asked for him, you got him, now you can take care of him."

Putting thoughts of bed and bath on hold, she pushed herself to her feet and went into the house. Quickly she washed up and changed into a pair of black sweatpants and an old, gray College of

205

William and Mary sweatshirt. Next she went to the kitchen, and made a stack of sandwiches and a pot of coffee. These she carried down to the stable and put in Ry's office.

Bobby and Marlin had set up cots outside Rough Cut's stall and sat on them, taking a well-deserved break. They sent Maggie weary smiles of appreciation when she offered them each a cup of coffee from her tray.

"Any change?" she asked softly.

They shook their heads.

"There are sandwiches down in Ry's office. Go help yourselves."

She stepped into the doorway of the stall. Christian and Dr. Maclay sat back against one wall, the trainer trying to rub a cramp out of his neck. Ry was bent over the stallion's head, dribbling cool water on him with a sponge. He glanced up at her and frowned.

"I thought I told you to go to bed."

"Yes, darlin', you did," she said. She served Styrofoam cups of steaming coffee to Christian and the vet, then offered the last one to Ry.

He took it and scowled at her. "Then why aren't you in bed?"

Deciding the best way to avoid an argument was to ignore him, she changed the subject. "How's he doing? He seems quieter. Is that good?"

Ry heaved a sigh, running his hand along the big ᵣse's cheek. Feeling as if he'd just turned two

206

hundred, he pushed himself to his feet. "He's getting worn out from fighting it. His temp's down a point, but that's still too high. I feel so damn helpless."

Maggie led him out of the stall. They sat down on one of the cots Bobby and Marlin had vacated to go in search of the sandwiches. She reached up and brushed a wayward lock of dark hair from Ry's forehead. "You're doing everything you can. Dr. Maclay said giving him that injection when you did may have saved his life."

May have saved his life, Ry thought. But what kind of life was it going to be? Potomac fever left its victims severely lame. Only days ago this horse had outperformed some of the top equine athletes in the world. Now, if he lived, it would be painful for him to walk out into his paddock. It seemed so unfair. This horse had been such a courageous champion. He had earned better than to be lame the rest of his life.

Permanent lameness was not the only damage this disease would do. It would also leave a stallion sterile. If they managed to pull him through the crisis, Rough Cut wasn't going to be worth his weight in dog food. There would be no syndication. All the plans that had been laid, all the improvements that had been made to the farm, all the money that had been spent on advertising would be considered a wasted effort. Instead of hauling money to the bank in a wheelbarrow,

Ry would be digging into his pocket to pay bills.

It was amazing how quickly things could change. Just a few long hours ago he had been riding home with Maggie in his arms, thinking of the future they would have together, the love he could give her, the security he could offer her. Now he could offer her only himself and his newfound love, and experience had taught him that wasn't enough.

Rough Cut's condition fluctuated between bad and worse every few hours. When morning came Bobby and Marlin were relieved by two other grooms. During one of the stallion's more stable periods, Christian slipped out to his cottage for a few hours of sleep. Dr. Maclay left, promising to return by noon. Ry had yet to leave the horse alone for more than five minutes.

Maggie had camped out near the stall on a lounge chair for part of the night, returning to the house near dawn. At seven-thirty she was on her way to the stable again, this time with doughnuts, fresh fruit, and a fresh pot of coffee.

Ry tossed down another cup of coffee but refused to eat a thing. He washed up in the bathroom off the lounge and changed into the clean shirt Maggie had brought out for him, then returned to the stall. His concentration was focused solely on saving Rough Cut's life. Regardless of what would happen afterward, he felt he owed it to the animal to do everything he could to save him. So he sat in the stall hour after hour, checking vital signs, administering medication when necessary, changing the IV bag when the need arose, sponging the horse down to help reduce his fever. Time passed without notice. He lost track of morning and afternoon.

Maggie helped as much as she could—more than he expected her to. Ry watched her push aside her fear, roll up her sleeves, and get right down in the stall with him to help bathe the horse, to stroke Rough Cut's head and try to comfort him when shots had to be given. He watched her work beside him, knowing she was working outside the stall as well, keeping the help fed, answering the phone, running errands. She had said she wanted to help, that this was to be her farm too.

Guilt poked at him when he realized Maggie didn't know what the ramifications of this illness would be. He was taking advantage of her ignorance. Rough Cut wasn't going to be their meal ticket, and she wasn't going to want anything to do with the farm or him when she found out where this illness was going to leave them.

He knew he had to tell her, but he put it off. He rationalized he couldn't leave the stallion, but he knew part of the reason he didn't tell her—a big part—was the comfort he took in having her near. It seemed every time his strength started to flag, there was Maggie with a soft touch, a word of encouragement, a cup of coffee. He had gotten used to having her around. If Fate had been kinder, he could have looked forward to that for the rest of his life. Instead, Fate had dealt his future a nasty blow. So, fair or not, he would keep Maggie with him through the worst of this crisis, because, Lord help him, he needed her. And when it was over he would let her go.

The morning of the third day Maggie approached Rough Cut's stall with a purposeful stride. Dr. Maclay and Christian Atherton stood in the aisle.

"How is he?"

Dr. Maclay ran a hand across his chin and sighed. "His condition has stabilized. His temperature is down to a hundred and three. He's not completely out of the woods, but I think the worst of it has passed."

Maggie gave a decisive nod, then turned on her heel, went into the stall, and grabbed Rylan by the shirt collar.

"Mary Margaret, what the hell!"

"You are coming with me, Rylan Quaid," she said in a tone that brooked no disobedience. When he came to his feet, she started out of the stall, tugging him along behind her with two fingers through a belt loop on his jeans. "You've been with this horse for thirty-six hours. You deserve a break, a meal, a shower, a shave, and some sleep—not necessarily in that order."

"I can't leave now," he protested, digging in his heels, effectively halting Maggie.

She glared over her shoulder at him. "You'll leave now if I have to take a riding crop to you. You aren't going to be any good to Rough Cut if you drop from exhaustion."

Christian hid his laughter discreetly behind his hand. Dr. Maclay waved them on. "Go on, Ry, Maggie's right. Take a break. Christian and I will keep watch here."

"Jeepers cripes," Ry muttered as they walked away from the stall. Hell, they were probably right. He felt as if he were at the rocky end of a long hard fall.

Maggie slid her arm around his waist, needing to touch him even if he did smell like a horse. "Now, don't scold me, Rylan. I'm worried about you. You haven't slept, you haven't eaten." Her voice caught as the strain of the last few days crashed down on her. "I–I know you're worried about C-Cutter, but—"

"Hey, hey, what's this all about?" he asked, stopping by the door to his office. He turned her to face him and tilted her chin up with his knuckles. Tears dampened her lashes, turning them into glistening dark spikes around her sable eyes.

She forced a rueful smile and reached up to brush the drops of moisture away. "I'm a big help."

"You are," he said seriously. "You've been working as hard as anybody."

And all for nothing. The thought dug into his conscience like a set of talons. He'd kept her there under false pretenses, working like a dog, for his own selfish reasons. He stood staring down at her, at her pale face and the dark smudges beneath her eyes. He had to tell her the truth, and he might as well do it now, when he was already feeling beaten.

"Come in the office, Maggie," he said, opening the door. "We need to talk."

"Ry, it can wait," she protested. "You need—"

"To talk to you, Maggie."

A strange apprehension closed around her heart like a fist. He seemed so businesslike all of a sudden. He wasn't wearing his normal scowl. His look was almost blank, oddly guarded. She had to fight the urge to turn and run before she stepped through the door ahead of him. Nerves kept her away from the chair in front of his desk. She didn't want to sit. Somehow she thought if she kept moving, the whole situation would lighten up. If she sat in that chair across from Ry like a truant student across from the principal, something bad was going to happen; she could sense it.

She wandered around the room she had spent so much time in the past week, stopping every few steps to stare at something without seeing it, then moving on.

Ry sank down on the big chair behind his desk—the chair Maggie had given him. Elbows on the blotter, he made a steeple of his fingers and watched her flit around the room like a skittish butterfly. He had dreaded this moment and postponed it further by saying nothing. Watching Maggie wander around his office was much preferable to watching her walk out the door.

When she could stand the silence no longer, Maggie said, "I suppose we'll have to postpone the open house. Is that what you wanted to talk to me about, sugar? I can—"

"It'll have to be canceled," he said flatly. He picked up an ink pen and rolled it between his palms.

"Canceled?" She stopped and looked at him, bewildered. "But why? We've done so much work getting ready. Why can't we just put it off for a couple of weeks? Cutter will be back to normal by then, won't he? And the investors—"

"There aren't going to be any investors, Maggie." He put down the pen and sighed, feeling as though he didn't have the strength to pick it back up. "If we manage to pull Rough Cut through this, he'll be sterile, useless as a sire or as anything else for that matter."

No wonder he looked so grim. Maggie's heart ached for him. Rough Cut was the horse he had worked all his life to raise. The stallion was to have been the cornerstone for the future of the farm. Now that dream was wrecked. "I see," she said quietly.

"Do you?" He pushed his chair back and stood, frustration forcing him to pace back and forth behind his desk. "Do you see that everything I've worked toward for the last few years is gone? Just like that the slate is wiped clean. Do you see that I've invested over a hundred thousand dollars on new facilities that won't even begin to pay for themselves now?" His voice rose a decibel with each statement as the anger built. "I invested money that was supposed to come from Rough Cut's syndication, but now there won't be any syndication, and I can't sell him off as a field hunter, because he'll be lame for the rest of his life! Do you see that I'm not only back to square one, I'm in the hole, Maggie."

"I understand what's happened is terrible, but it's not the end of the world, Ry. Rough Cut isn't the only good horse you've got. You've got stables full of fine animals. Why can't we go on with the open house and simply change the emphasis? We could show off the young stock. The new facilities are wonderful; there's no reason we shouldn't—"

"*We* won't do anything." He dropped back down on his chair, cradling his head in his hands as he leaned on the desktop once more. Damn, he was tired, and things were going to get worse before there was any hope of their getting better. "I'll take care of calling the investors. I'll take care of canceling the open house. It's my responsibility. I've imposed on you too much as it is."

"Imposed?" She stopped in front of his desk. He looked exhausted. A three-day stubble darkened the harsh planes of his face. His hair was mussed from too many finger combings. He looked tough and angry and hurt. Maggie propped a hip on the desk and leaned across to stroke her fingertips down his beard-roughened cheek. "Sugar, it's no imposition. We're in this together."

His hand closed around her wrist, and he removed her touch from his face. This was bad enough without being reminded of how soft she was, how tender she could be. Heaven help him, if he got a whiff of her perfume, he wasn't going to be able to go through with what he had to do.

"Don't, Maggie. Don't you see what this means? I promised you I could give you things, that I could give you everything you ever wanted. Now I won't have anything left to give you except bills and headaches. I don't expect you to hang around."

"You don't expect . . ." She let the words trail off as their awful meaning tried to penetrate. That fist of apprehension tightened. Her heart pounded as Ry went on.

"I made an offer I can no longer make good on, so the deal's off. I'm sorry, Mary Margaret. I wish it could have been different."

215

"You're throwing in the towel," she said, pulling her wrist from his grasp and rubbing it absently as she stared at him in disbelief.

He looked away.

Fuming, she pushed herself to her feet. "You're throwing in the towel. I ought to strangle you with it. You and your confounded deals! Do you really think I ever gave a hoot in hell about the money?"

The look on his face told her plainly what he'd thought.

"You son of a gun." She ground the words out through clenched teeth. "I suppose I should be flattered that you thought so little of me but were still willing to marry me. Or didn't it matter to you? I guess you made it plain enough the first time you asked me to marry you—what you wanted was a brood mare. As long as I was genetically compatible, maybe it didn't matter that I was so lacking in character that I would marry you for your money."

"Stop it, Maggie!" He came out of his chair once again, fists clenched at his sides.

She glared at him. "Have you never once believed me when I told you I loved you?"

"You thought you were in love with a man who was about to come into a lot of money. I never held that against you. I can understand—"

"You wouldn't understand an anvil if it fell on your head. Choke on your damn money, Rylan

Quaid. I never wanted a nickel of it. Never." She stepped back from the desk, retreating as her anger shifted and let the pain through. "All I ever wanted was you, though Lord only knows why. I guess in my dreams you were never such a hardheaded, hard-hearted bastard. The man of my dreams would never have accused me of wanting him for his money." She tried to swallow back her tears as she said, "In my dreams you loved me back."

"I do, Maggie." The words came out in a strangled whisper. He could hardly look at her, it hurt so much. He loved her, but love had never been enough to keep a woman in his life before, and he had nothing more to offer her. She was hurt now, but he was doing her a favor, and he was doing himself one. Better to hurt her pride now than to wait for that inevitable day when she would tire of the farm, the bills . . . him. But he couldn't let her go thinking he had never cared. For the first time in a long time he had cared. He had cared too much.

Maggie shook her head, her brown eyes full of accusation and pain and disillusionment. Her voice trembled when she spoke. "No. If you loved me, you'd believe me when I said those words to you. You wouldn't bend them and twist them and throw them back at me and tell me they're just a pretty cover for greed. You'd know that I've been out here night and day because I'm worried sick about you, not because I wanted to keep an eye on the big investment.

"You can take that horse and ride him straight to hell. I never wanted anything more than your love, Rylan. When you're ready to accept that, you come and see me."

She bolted out of the office and ran for her car, not caring that she was leaving behind two suitcases worth of clothing and cosmetics. That was the least of what she was leaving behind, she thought as she drove down the tree-lined lane with tears streaming down her face. She was leaving behind a broken dream and a broken heart.

Why had she had to pick Rylan Quaid to fall in love with? The world was full of men who had no ghosts haunting them, men who recognized love for what it was. Why was this man, this man who had learned not to trust, the one who haunted her dreams?

And why had she had to pick a tourist attraction for her home? she wondered as she pulled into the parking area at Poplar Grove. It was a beautiful day and it appeared every tourist traveling through Virginia was taking advantage of the weather, touring not only the house, but the lovely grounds of the old plantation as well.

Maggie dug through her glove compartment, throwing out maps, a mitten, crumpled notes, and a petrified candy bar as she searched for a pair of sunglasses to hide her tear-ravaged face. The ones she found had one bow missing, but she put them on anyway.

Lord, she thought, glancing at her reflection in the car window when she got out, she looked like a vagrant. She was wearing one of Rylan's flannel shirts with the sleeves rolled up. The tails hung to just above her knees—not quite long enough to cover the frayed hole in her oldest jeans. Dirty sneakers and the one-armed sunglasses completed her outfit.

Oh, well, she thought, looking like a bag lady was another good reason for her to sneak into the house without letting anyone see her. Her emotions were rubbed raw. The last thing she wanted was to come within fifty feet of another human being—especially one that might ask personal questions.

In the safety of her room Maggie let the tears come. She pulled off the shirt she had borrowed from Ry and curled up on the bed sobbing into the soft, worn flannel until exhaustion claimed her and she fell asleep only to dream of the man she loved but would never have.

ten

"YOU CALL THAT a grooming job? Cripes, I've seen horses come out of dust storms with better looking coats than that!" Ry barked at the young groom.

The groom, a slight young man with a shock of spiky wheat-colored hair, jumped back a step from his employer. Behind him, the horse with the controversial coat snorted and rolled his eyes. Dancing nervously in the cross ties, the chestnut's shoes scraped against the cement floor.

Ry snatched the brush out of the groom's hands and shook it at him. "Do it again. If that horse ain't shining like a bald man's head on a hot July day by the time I come back, so help me, I'll sweep the floor with you."

"Yessir!"

"You'll be mucking out stalls until the Second Coming. You got that?"

"Yessir!"

"I believe," a soft low voice drawled behind Ry, "that beating stable hands is against the law in the commonwealth of Virginia."

Ry let out a pent-up breath and forced his shoulders to relax. He handed the brush back to the groom, then turned to look down at his little sister. Katie stared up at him with her pewter-gray eyes, her fists propped on her slim hips. Her expression was a complex mix of emotions— love, concern, reproach, gentle teasing.

"Hi, princess," he said. He brushed a kiss across her cheek and walked out of the barn. Katie fell in step beside him, her flowered skirt swirling softly around her legs as they walked. Ry glanced at his sister from the corner of his eye. "I wasn't gonna beat him," he said dryly. "Maybe just shake him some by the scruff of his neck."

Katie shook her head. The end of her chestnut braid twitched above her waist as she climbed the stairs to the front porch. "So Christian wasn't exaggerating. He stopped in the restaurant the other day when Nick and I were having lunch and told us you were terrorizing the hired help."

Ry scowled, as he held the front door open for her. "I pay him to ride horses, not to be the damn town crier."

"You ought to pay him for being your friend," Katie said sarcastically. "The men who follow the elephants in parades have a more enjoyable job."

His dour look was wasted on the back of her head as she preceded him into the den. She didn't take a seat on any of the sturdy chairs but wandered the room that was filled with trophies, many of which she had won before her accident.

"Did you drive all the way out here to tell me I have a lousy disposition?" Ry asked. Going to the long table that stood behind the sofa, he picked up a nutcracker and played with it absently.

"No," Katie said. "That's hardly a news flash. Is there some reason I can't visit my family home on a Saturday afternoon and spend some time with my only brother?"

He knew exactly why she had come and thought it best to head her off at the pass. "Katie, if you're here to talk about Maggie and me—"

"Why would I be here to talk about you and Maggie?" One delicately arched brow winged upward in sardonic question. "Just because she's wasting away with a broken heart, and you're fit to kill somebody?"

"I've got plenty of reason to be on a short fuse these days."

"Yes." She sighed and perched herself on the arm of the sofa. "I know you do. How's Cutter?"

"Better. He's still weak . . . still worthless. Nothing's going to change that."

"You'll keep him though, won't you?" It was more a statement than a question.

"You know he's more than earned a retirement home here."

"Yes, he has, but not everyone would see it that way."

"I'm not everyone."

"That's for sure. You're definitely one of a kind, big brother." Katie's soft husky laugh faded along with her smile. "I love you. I hate to see people I love in pain."

Ry put the nutcracker down and walked to the window with his back to his sister. "Katie, don't start this."

In his mind's eye he could see the sad smile that curved her wide mouth when she spoke.

"We've had this conversation before, haven't we? This is the other side of the coin, I guess."

He remembered the scene she was recalling. He

had gone to her house and practically bullied her into going to see Nick when she had wanted to end their relationship. He had been all full of big talk that day, telling Katie she was pushing happiness away, that she was being a coward.

"I reckon you owe me an earful after that, don't you?" he said with a rueful twist to his lips.

"I want to see you happy, Ry."

"I'm doing okay."

Katie raised his eyebrows with a two-syllable opinion of his statement. "You're miserable and making everyone who works for you miserable too. It's a wonder they haven't all quit. Why are you doing this to yourself, to Maggie? She loves you. Ry."

He turned to face her, calling up the argument he had used on Maggie, the one he had used on himself at least twice a day since she'd left. "I made her promises I can't keep, Katie."

"That's a load, brother. She loves you. She doesn't care if you're a prince or a pauper."

"Maybe today she doesn't. Maybe today she thinks it would be romantic to marry me and be in hock up to her ears, but what about tomorrow or next year or the year after that?" he asked, emotion raising his voice.

Backing off, he turned and slowly paced back and forth in front of one of the trophy shelves, his big hands hitched to the waistband of his worn jeans. "I had my shot at putting this farm on top, and now it's back in the hole, I practically have to start over again. You know as well as I do, a horse like Rough Cut comes along once in a lifetime, if you're lucky. I've had my luck, and now it's run out." Finally he gave voice to the fear that had stayed buried in his heart all these years. His voice trembled with the emotion it took to release the thought. "What's to keep Maggie from doing the same?"

Katie's eyes were full of compassion and empathy. "She's not Mama, Ry," she said softly. "Christian told me Maggie stayed out in the barn with you day and night when Cutter was sick. Do you think Mama would have done that? She hated this place. I can't remember her ever setting foot in the stables. Christian told me Maggie got down on her hands and knees in that filthy stall and helped you take care of that sick horse."

He gave her a black look. "He's a regular gosh darn fountain of information, isn't he? Didn't Mary Margaret tell you all that herself?"

"No," Katie said softly, holding his gaze with a very serious look. "Maggie hasn't had a lot to say the last few weeks."

The pain that statement caused him was surprisingly sharp, so sharp it stopped him in his tracks directly in front of Katie. Mary Margaret always bounced back. How many times over the last few weeks had he pictured her tilting her head and batting her lashes at some other man? He had never pictured her suffering, probably because he couldn't bear the thought of her tears.

Katie went on. "Not even you are cynical enough to believe she did all that because she expected to get some kind of payback."

"No, I guess I'm not," he murmured. That kind of cynicism had protected him once. It had allowed him to hold his emotions in check and keep his heart out of reach. Acknowledging his love for Maggie had taken that shield away from him. No matter how hard he'd tried over the last weeks, he hadn't quite been able to pull it back into place.

"Ry," Katie said, catching his hand and holding it tight. "You once told me that I was letting the past control my life. Aren't you doing the same?"

His jaw clenched as he looked away from her.

"You told me to take a chance on happiness. Why don't you?"

Because I'm terrified, he admitted to himself. Because every time he had taken a chance in the past he had ended up getting hurt. Because he had decided a long time ago it was better to be alone than hurting.

He had built a nice safe life on the farm, giving his love to his animals because they never tried to throw it back at him. He had been fool enough to think he could add Maggie to that life without risking anything. Now he was facing the threat he had vowed never to face again, and it scared the living hell out of him. He was a big, tough man, a man who feared very few things, but this had him shaking right down to his soul.

"I won't give her my heart then watch her walk away with it."

"Haven't you done that already?"

He turned and walked to the window again and stared out at the blue mountains that rose to the west. Katie was right. He had ended the relationship before Maggie had a chance to, but it had already been too late. He had given her his heart, then driven her away. Now he was only half alive, lashing out in pain at everyone around him. He was such miserable company, even the stray dogs avoided him these days.

"Rylan, Maggie has stuck with you through all the grief you've given her the past three months. She'll probably stick with you through anything," Katie said. "So you're not going to be rich now. Wouldn't you rather know she was staying with you out of love? Money runs out, Ry, love never does."

"It has before," he said in a low, hoarse voice. "More than once."

"No, not real love. There are lots of imitations, and they never last, but Maggie loves you. The real thing, big brother. Wouldn't you rather take a chance on that than live in this big old house all alone for the rest of your life? Being safe has its good points, but you and I both know it can get lonely living behind the walls we build to protect our hearts."

When he felt his sister's arms slip around his waist, Ry turned and hugged her, startled as always by how tiny and fragile she was but not startled in the least by how much he loved her.

"Think about it," she said, looking up at him. "I have to go. As you may have guessed, I only came out here to browbeat you. I would have come out sooner, but I've been too involved in my research."

"Historical details for one of your houses?" he asked as he walked her to the door.

"No. Adoption details."

He couldn't have been more surprised. Katie's inability to give Nick children had nearly put an end to their relationship. She almost had let him go because of it, and because she had been afraid to face the option open to her.

"It scares the heck out of me," she said with a little laugh as she stepped out onto the porch, "but I at least need to check into it, if for no other reason than to prove I'm not going to let the past rule my future."

"What does Nick have to say about it?"

She smiled with all the warmth that was in her heart at the mention of her husband. "He'll stick by me one way or the other. That's what love's all about, Ry. Take it from me, it's pretty terrific."

He watched Katie drive out of the yard just as it started to rain. Staring out at the deserted yard, he stood in the doorway listening to the lonely sound of rain on the tin roof of the porch. Finally he turned and went back into the dark, silent house and wandered from room to room until he reached his own bedroom, the room he had shared with Maggie, the room he had lain awake in night after night since she'd left.

The day she'd gone he had searched through the closet and removed all the clothes and shoes she'd left behind—the blouses and slacks she had hung beside his shirts and jeans, the tiny sneakers and leather flats she had lined up beside his size thirteen cowboy boots. He had rummaged through the cupboard in the bathroom, removing every toiletry article that belonged to her—the bottles and tubes of makeup, the flowery-scented bath powder she liked, the pink-handled razor she had placed on the shelf beside his shaving gear. He had packed up everything and sent a groom to Poplar Grove to deliver the stuff.

Even so, he was still finding remnants of Maggie—a lace-trimmed anklet in with his athletic socks, a barrette forgotten on the night-stand, a frilly garter belt that had somehow found its way under the bed. Every time he found a little reminder of her it was like catching a glimpse of her in a crowd, then losing her again. Lord, he missed her. How empty the house was with her gone and only the faint memory of her perfume lingering in the air.

Passion's Promise. He wandered to his dresser and picked up the tiny cut-glass bottle of perfume he had found tucked behind his aftershave. Maggie was full of passion. So was he when he was with her. Without her he felt old and empty, like this house.

This old house had seen so little happiness over the years. Then, for a few short days it had been filled with passion's promise, the promise of love and laughter and the ring of children's voices. A promise unfulfilled. A promise that was still within his reach if only he dared take the chance.

Did he dare risk his heart? Hell, he'd already done that. Did he want Mary Margaret McSwain to share his life? Damn right, he did. She was the only woman he'd ever wanted to share his future with. Maybe that future wasn't as bright as it had been a few weeks ago, but it wasn't exactly bleak either. Maggie had seen that. He could hear her talking about the directions they could go with the farm now that Rough Cut was out of the picture. She had been willing to stick with him, even though he hadn't believed in her at the time.

Maggie McSwain was one hell of a lady. She was the lady he loved, the lady he wanted, needed, had to have by his side for the rest of his life.

Then what was he doing standing around

gawking like a half-wit? He had plans to make, things to do, people to see.

Resolve straightened him to his full height. It hardened his expression and curled his big hands into fists—one of which automatically squeezed the atomizer of the perfume bottle he was holding, sending a cloud of Passion's Promise across his massive chest.

Scowling, Ry looked down and sniffed as the stuff soaked into his shirt and skin. "Well, hell."

He came to her out of the mist. Tall, rugged, his face lined with strain, his smoky green eyes filled with regret and longing. She stood on the veranda, waiting for him, as she had waited for him all her life. She leaned against a pillar, her hands pressed to the smooth cool surface. The wind rose, swirling the mists around them both and tugging at the hem of her long gown.

Halting his horse at the foot of the steps, he said, "Maggie, I love you. I need you. I need your love."

"Do you believe in me, Ry? Do you believe I could love you?"

"Yes. I'll believe in your love always. I'll love you forever."

She stepped away from the pillar and reached out to him. Then she was on the horse with him, in front of him with his strong arms around her and his heart beating beneath her ear. He bent his head

230

and kissed her. Then he turned the horse toward the hills, and the mists swallowed them up.

Maggie jerked awake, then lay still in bed listening to the wind howl outside the old plantation house. It was raining. The colorless light falling in through her window was testimony to that, as was the sound of water splattering against the mullioned panes. Slowly she sat up, tucking her knees and the covers under her chin. She looked across the room to the corner Randy the bear had been relegated to.

"Another day, another *hic* headache, huh, Randy?"

The enormous stuffed brown bear stared back at her.

She rubbed two fingers over the dull throb in each temple. She had lost track of the number of nights she had fallen asleep with tears on her cheeks, then awakened from the same dream with her head pounding. The cycle was taking its toll on her, physically and emotionally. Her usually sunny disposition had become as gloomy and blustery as the late fall weather. A glance in the mirror as she forced herself to get out of bed confirmed her suspicions that she looked like hell.

If the bags under her eyes drooped any farther, they were going to be on her chest. The lines of strain she had seen on Ry's face in her dream were, in reality, drawn on her own face. On the up side, those ten extra pounds she had been unable to shed since adolescence had melted away. Too bad she didn't care enough to be happy about that.

Wrapping her black kimono around her, Maggie stared out the window and sighed. This had to end. She had to accept the fact that her dream would never come true. She loved Ry, but he wasn't able or willing to believe in that love. Her struggle to free him from his past had been in vain. In the end he had managed to stay behind those walls he had built to protect himself. He might live the rest of his life behind them, safe but alone, while she was free to pick up the pieces of her heart and try again, or at least go on with her life.

A month had passed since their last encounter. There had been no phone call. He hadn't come to see her. She hadn't run into him on the street in Briarwood. The only place she saw him was in her dreams, but that man wasn't real. He had never been real. It was time to let the dream die.

Despite the unpleasant weather, a fair number of tourists made their way out to Poplar Grove in the afternoon. The rain abated, leaving behind a thin fog that seemed to seep into everything. For once Maggie was glad of the layers of petticoats she wore under her costume. The low-scooping décolletage was another matter, one she solved by wrapping a soft blue woolen shawl around her shoulders.

A two-hundred-year-old plantation house

shrouded in mist on a windy November day was really quite romantic, Maggie thought. Not that she appreciated that sort of thing these days. Inside, fires burned in all the working fireplaces, creating a wonderful ambiance for the visitors. Ladies in colonial garb led guests through the shadowed house and told them romantic tales of days gone by. It wasn't such a bad way to spend a Sunday afternoon.

She thought of all the Sunday afternoons that stretched out before her and felt a wave of melancholy coming on. *No, no, you don't, McSwain,* she told herself. *You're through pining over Rylan Quaid.*

But what was he doing today? Was he lonely? Did he miss her? Was he sitting in his study with the lights off, staring out at the mountains, thinking about her? If the phone rang, would he hope it might be she?

She shook herself out of her trance, a blush heating her cheeks more than the dining room fireplace did. The entire tour group was staring at her. "I'm sorry," she said, "I seem to be a bit distracted today."

At the end of the tour, she thanked her guests and directed them to the old kitchen across the forecourt, where they were to help themselves to hot apple cider. Her duties completed, she stepped out onto the porch and began contemplating the nerve-soothing aspect of losing touch with reality.

She pulled her shawl close around her, leaned against a pillar, and stared out through the fog that was as sheer as gauze.

Suddenly a dot appeared between the trees at the end of the driveway, a dark brown dot that became a blob in the fog as it drew closer. Then it was a blob with legs. Then it was blob with legs and foot-long ears.

"Oh, my Lord, it's a mule!" Maggie said, as if a mule was the most horrible thing she had ever seen.

Curious tourists filed out of the house and outbuildings as the creature let loose a bray loud enough to wake the dead in the next county. It was a mule, all right, and it wasn't alone. Maggie's jaw dropped as the animal emerged from another layer of fog. The mule's rider held a bouquet of dilapidated roses and wore a scowl that was blacker than a moonless night.

"Rylan!" Maggie exclaimed, pushing herself away from the pillar. She rushed to the top of the porch steps and stared, aghast.

He was splattered with mud from head to toe. There was a rip in the knee of his jeans. He glared at the mule as he slid from its back. It brayed again, the sound echoing all around the grounds. Ry stomped to the foot of the stairs and thrust the roses at Maggie.

"Here. The mule thought they were for him."

Maggie accepted the bouquet, tears flooding her

eyes. Ry had brought her flowers! So what if half the buds and leaves had been chewed off by a mule? This was the most romantic thing Rylan Quaid had ever done. Maybe there was hope for him after all.

"Oh, Rylan, I'm sure they were lovely . . . before the mule ate them. By the way, why are you riding a mule?"

He snorted in disgust and planted his hands on his hips. "Jeepers cripes, I was on my way over here and had a blowout on the pickup, and the blasted spare was flatter than my Aunt Martha. So I walked about eighty-five miles to Rueben's, and the best he could do was loan me that jackass."

"Mr. Quaid, your language!" Mrs. Claiborne sniffed from behind Maggie.

"I would have called Christian and had him come and get me, but Reuben doesn't have a phone," he went on sarcastically. "He thinks phones are the instruments of Satan. That's why I'm riding a mule, Mary Margaret. Do you want to make something of it?"

Maggie frowned at him. "No. I think it's very appropriate for you to go around on a jackass. Like minds should travel together."

He narrowed his eyes. "Very amusing. Aren't you just a little curious as to what I'm doing here?"

Curious wasn't the word. There wasn't a word in any known language to describe what she was feeling. She hadn't seen or heard from him in weeks. When they'd parted, she had told him not to come near her until he was ready to accept the fact that she loved him no matter what he was, rich or poor, charming or irascible. And here he was. It was like a bizarre variation of her dream. He had ridden in on a lop-eared mule instead of a beautiful horse, and he was scowling instead of pledging his love. But he had brought her flowers.

Her heart was in her throat as she raised her eyes from the roses to meet Rylan's gaze. All her sassy bravado vanished. Beneath her long skirts, her legs were shaking like a pair of jackhammers. She could almost hear the tourists and the Darlington sisters holding their breath as she asked softly, "Why are you here, Rylan?"

"I need you, Maggie."

Holding his gaze, she shook her head ever so slightly, like a pitcher shaking off the catcher's signals in a baseball game. "I need you" wasn't what she had to hear.

Ry shuffled his feet, his boots crunching on the gravel path. "I love you, Maggie. I need you in my life," he said quietly.

When she only stared at him, her expression unchanged, his anger flared up. His dark brows lowered ominously over his glittering eyes, making him look like a dangerous predatory animal as he took an aggressive step toward the porch. "Dammit, Mary Margaret, I'm miserable without you. I love you, I want you. Now I'm gonna ask you one last time, will you marry me or not?"

She held back her smile as she looked at him scowling up at her. "Maybe," she said.

He looked ready to slug somebody. "What the Sam Hill kind of an answer is that? Maybe?"

Setting her roses aside, she descended the steps and stood in front of him, only inches away, gazing up into his rugged face. "Do you believe in me, Ry? Do you believe I love you, that I've loved you forever? Do you believe I'll love you no matter what happens with the farm?"

He swallowed hard, his shield of orneriness deserting him, leaving the vulnerability naked in his eyes. He felt as if his whole life were riding on his answer. As he looked down at her, he thought of all they had been through in the last few months—all he had put her through. And she had stuck with him. Katie said that was what love was all about.

"I believe you love me, Maggie," he said, putting his big hands on her shoulders. "Marry me and prove you'll love me forever. Honest to God, I don't think I can live without you."

She reached up and brushed a streak of mud from his cheek. How dear he was to her, big, rough Rylan Quaid. He didn't write her love sonnets. He'd never kissed the back of her hand. The only flowers he'd ever given her had been chomped on by a mule. But she'd been right about one thing all along. Inside that tough, ornery hide of his was a man who needed love, a man who had love to give. He might not have been down on bended knee, but he was offering that love to her with his heart in his eyes.

She could have walked away about as easily as she could have stopped breathing.

"Yes, I'll marry you," she whispered.

Ry breathed a sigh of relief that left him feeling dizzy. He threw his arms around Maggie and pulled her against him, nearly crushing her in his embrace. He buried his face in her dark copper hair and breathed in the scent of her shampoo and a whiff of Passion's Promise. "Gosh almighty, Mary Margaret, it took you long enough to answer!"

Polite applause sounded around them.

Maggie peeked out at the tourists, then glanced sheepishly up at Ry, tears twinkling in her eyes. "They think we're part of the tour."

He chuckled and grinned at her. "Maybe we should pass the hat for tips. We could use the money."

"Oh, pooh, sugar." Maggie tilted her head and batted her lashes at him. Winding her arms around his neck, she raised up on tiptoe and hugged him. "What do I need with money when I've got the man of my dreams?"

about the author

Bestselling author Tami Hoag's novels have appeared regularly on national bestseller lists since the publication of her first book in 1988. She lives in Los Angeles. Her website is www.tamihoag.com.

Center Point Large Print
600 Brooks Road / PO Box 1
Thorndike ME 04986-0001 USA

(207) 568-3717

US & Canada:
1 800 929-9108
www.centerpointlargeprint.com